"My feelings for you haven't changed."

"You can't seriously believe that's true," Melody said.

"I want you in my life. I want to be there for our baby. How do you see your future?"

"Honestly, I sort of go back and forth—wanting us to be a happy family but thinking it might be better if I raise this baby on my own."

"Because..." If he asked her whether she was in love with someone else and she told him yes, Kyle wasn't sure what he'd do.

"Because it hurts too much when I think how much I love you and wonder if you'll ever feel the same about me."

* * *

The Heir Affair is part of the Las Vegas Nights series: An exclusive club for men who have it all and want more.

Dear Reader,

I'm excited to be bringing you the last book in my Las Vegas Nights series centered around Club T's. Since I first started writing Savannah and Trent's book, *The Black Sheep's Secret Child*, I've been excited to share Melody and Kyle's story. With my daughter heading off to college next year, I've been thinking a lot about how hard it can be to maintain relationships over a long distance. And with public figures spending so much time in the spotlight, sometimes the most innocent of situations can be misinterpreted.

It's been fun revisiting my Las Vegas Nights world and bringing in characters from the first three books. I hope you enjoy Melody and Kyle's story.

All the best,

Cat Schield

CAT SCHIELD

———

THE HEIR AFFAIR

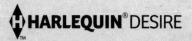

Recycling programs
for this product may
not exist in your area.

ISBN-13: 978-0-373-83868-4

The Heir Affair

Copyright © 2017 by Catherine Schield

Printed in U.S.A.

Cat Schield has been reading and writing romance since high school. Although she graduated from college with a BA in business, her idea of a perfect career was writing books for Harlequin. And now, after winning the Romance Writers of America 2010 Golden Heart® Award for Best Contemporary Series Romance, that dream has come true. Cat lives in Minnesota with her daughter, Emily, and their Burmese cat. When she's not writing sexy, romantic stories for Harlequin Desire, she can be found sailing with friends on the St. Croix River, or in more exotic locales, like the Caribbean and Europe. She loves to hear from readers. Find her at catschield.net and follow her on Twitter, @catschield.

Books by Cat Schield

Harlequin Desire

The Sherdana Royals

Royal Heirs Required
A Royal Baby Surprise
Secret Child, Royal Scandal

Las Vegas Nights

At Odds with the Heiress
A Merger by Marriage
A Taste of Temptation
The Black Sheep's Secret Child
Little Secret, Red Hot Scandal
The Heir Affair

Visit her Author Profile page at Harlequin.com, or catschield.net, for more titles!

To Patty and Fred

One

Kyle Tailor sat on the couch beside his business part-ner and best friend from high school, Trent Caldwell. It was Thanksgiving. On the great room's sixty-inch television, an interdivisional grudge match was happening between the Detroit Lions and Minnesota Vikings. Kyle wasn't following the action. His gaze was locked on Trent's sister.

Until she came along, solitude had never bothered him. In most ways it was simpler to live on his own without someone else's physical or emotional clutter. To find himself needing Melody had been a shock to his system.

Now, he didn't sleep well without her beside him. Since she'd been gone, he slogged through business meetings and routine activities in a foggy daze, unable to concentrate or care. He missed her hugs. Her way of teasing him. He'd lost weight, had stopped working out and lost an unacceptable amount of money in the casinos in the month since he'd come to Las Vegas to temporarily take over the management of Club T's.

Trent elbowed him in his ribs.

Kyle ripped his gaze from Melody and arched an eyebrow at his business partner. "What?"

"Go talk to her."

"I tried earlier." When he'd first arrived, they'd exchanged a stilted "Happy Thanksgiving" and an awkward half hug. "She's avoiding me."

"Did you perfect your world-famous curveball on your first attempt?" Trent countered. "Try again."

"She's on the phone."

Trent grunted and returned his attention to the television. His infant son sat on his lap. His matching blue eyes were on the screen and every time the Lions scored and Trent cheered, Dylan would respond to his father's enthusiasm with clapping. From the love seat, the child's mother watched the pair with such fondness Kyle's gut twisted.

Laughter rose from the kitchen. Nate Tucker, the third partner in their Las Vegas nightclub, was in the process of putting away the leftovers from dinner, helped by Mia Navarro, a fellow songwriter he'd been dating for several months.

Thanksgiving was a day for families. A chance to celebrate what they had. Nate had Mia. Trent had Savannah and Dylan.

Frustration ate at him. Kyle should have had Melody

except five months ago the paparazzi had captured her and famous DJ/music producer Hunter Graves coming out of a New York City nightclub hand-in-hand. The way Melody and her former flame had been smiling at each other had eaten at Kyle day and night until he'd accused her of cheating on him. Although she'd denied it, Kyle couldn't find a way to believe her.

After all, hadn't it been Hunter with whom she'd been so deeply in love that she was prepared to do almost anything to get him to love her back? Even engage in a crazy scheme to make Hunter realize he was taking her for granted. But playing like she was in love with Kyle to make Hunter jealous had become real awfully fast. That was probably why the plan had worked so well.

Seeing that he had real competition for Melody, Hunter had realized the error of his ways. But there was another outcome that neither Melody nor Kyle had seen coming. They'd actually fallen for each other. Kyle remembered back to the moment when all three of them had stood in her apartment, with Melody between the two men who loved her. The seconds were burned in his mind. Her choice could have gone either way. He'd experienced a heart-stopping range of emotions while he waited for her decision.

And in the months since, Kyle would be lying if he claimed he'd never wondered if she was happy with choosing him over Hunter.

His heart gave a sickening lurch as he regarded Melody. She was in great spirits at the moment. Her blue eyes sparkled. The corners of her mouth were turned up in a wry smile and her cheeks flushed with color.

Was she on the phone with Hunter Graves?

Disgusted with himself for jumping to that conclusion, Kyle turned to the television and forced his attention back to the game, but it was all just a swirl of purple, white and blue on a green background.

Falling in love with Melody had been the most incredible experience of his life. No woman before her had ever consumed his thoughts like this, and their lovemaking was exhilarating. Yet he had a hard time trusting the joy and found himself unable to shake the ever-present doubts that lurked in his subconscious, fears that nothing that felt so good could last forever.

Based on how his former love life had gone, he'd braced himself for the inevitable end of their relationship, prepared himself for loss. But the months stretched out and things between them had just gotten better. He'd loosened the reins of control and started to open up. And then she'd gone on tour and their physical separation had created an emotional gulf.

The damning photo of her and Hunter in New York had come at a point when too much time apart had demonstrated just how vulnerable their fledgling relationship was. Neither one of them had had enough confidence in their connection to weather such an emotionally charged situation. Pain pierced his temple. He dug his thumb into the spot.

There was another jab to his ribs. "She's off the phone."

"Thanks." Kyle got to his feet and headed for the terrace.

Melody was on her way in. They met at the sliding glass door. Kyle stepped into the opening, blocking her from reentering the house.

"Look," he said without preliminaries. "I came here tonight so we could talk."

"You didn't come for Nate's cooking?"

Kyle didn't crack a smile and Melody sighed in defeat. He knew she hated when he shut down like this, but he'd grown up building walls around his emotions. The strategy blocked pain and disappointment. Unfortunately, as his therapist liked to put it, it also kept him from "welcoming joy."

He'd started seeing Dr. Warner when his baseball career abruptly ended a few years earlier after a string of shoulder and elbow injuries led to surgery and he was unable to make a full recovery. Needing to see a shrink filled him with shame and embarrassment. In fact, he'd let himself sink into some pretty dark mental territory before he'd made his first appointment. But the fact was, he'd needed help. Losing a career he loved left him feeling more vulnerable than he knew how to handle.

His dad would say a real man would suck it up and deal with his problems instead of running to some head shrinker. In Brent Tailor's world, men didn't talk about all that touchy-feely crap. A real man made decisions and if things went wrong, he fixed them. Kyle often wondered if his father thought a real man didn't have feelings.

"We need to sort out what's going on between us," he said, stepping outside, herding her away from the family room and the safety of their friends.

"I don't know where to start."

"Your stuff is still at my place in LA, but you haven't been there since the tour ended. Are you coming back?"

"I don't know."

"It feels like we're over."

Melody's voice sounded rough as she asked, "Is that what you want?"

"No, but I can't remain in limbo, either. We either need to move forward or be done." Giving Melody this ultimatum hadn't been part of his plan tonight. He hadn't wanted to fight with her at all. "The decision is up to you."

"I need to think about it."

Impatience snapped along his nerve endings. "The tour ended two months ago. You've had plenty of time to think."

"Things are a little more complicated than they seem."

She didn't elaborate even though Kyle gave her the space to do so. Once upon a time Melody had been able to talk to Kyle about everything. Now, it was as if they were strangers.

"How complicated can it be?" he finally asked. "Do you want to be with me or with Hunter?"

"With Hunter?" She shook her head in bewilderment. "What are you talking about?"

"That was him on the phone a little while ago, wasn't it?"

"No. It was my mom calling to wish me a happy Thanksgiving." She paused and her expression grew incredulous as she stared at him. "Why would you think that it was Hunter?"

Kyle didn't respond right away. "He wants you back."

She huffed out a laugh. "That's ridiculous. Why would you think something like that?"

"He told me so."

"You spoke with him?" Melody looked aghast and confused that Kyle and Hunter had talked. "When?"

"After the two of you met up in New York. I called and warned him to back off. He told me to go screw myself." His fist clenched at the memory. "Apparently that night you said something to him about how being on the road can put a strain on a relationship." Kyle had no idea what had prompted Melody to divulge such private details to her ex-lover, but hearing Hunter repeat the confidence had cut deep. "He took that to mean we weren't getting along. And he told me he intends to make you fall back in love with him."

"He wouldn't do that."

"Don't you mean he can't do that?" Kyle blew out a breath and struggled to calm his pounding heart.

"Hunter can't get me back…" She didn't meet his gaze. "Because I still love you." An undertone of doubt marred the declaration.

"You don't sound as if you believe that."

Shivering, she glanced toward the sliding glass

door. When her eyes widened, Kyle followed the direction of her gaze and realized four pairs of eyes were watching them. As soon as their audience realized they'd been spotted, everyone looked away. Melody covered her face with her hands and groaned.

"They all want what's best for us," Kyle said.

Everyone in the house was pulling for them with the exception of one-year-old Dylan, who had no idea what was going on, and perhaps, Melody herself.

"I know." She let her hands fall. "I don't want to have this conversation here. Can you take me back to Trent's? We can continue our discussion there."

Getting her to talk to him was all he'd wanted these last few months. Well, maybe not *all* he'd wanted. If the tour had never happened. If she'd never gone to New York City and met up with Hunter in the nightclub. If he'd never let jealousy get the better of him. If he'd been allowed to express his emotions growing up.

His list of ifs went on and on.

But for now, he was happy that they were communicating again. Even if what was being said had the potential to hurt.

Kyle nodded. "That sounds good to me."

Ten minutes later, after they'd said their goodbyes, Kyle was negotiating the streets of Las Vegas, heading to the two-bedroom guesthouse on her brother's property where Melody stayed whenever she visited Las Vegas.

Kyle kept his attention fixed on the road, his hands tense on the wheel as if something was eating at him.

Every so often he flicked an unreadable glance her direction. It wasn't like him to look so grim around her. The Kyle she'd grown up with had been quick to smile and tease. Even though he'd been her brother's best friend, he'd treated her like she mattered to him. Mattered to him like a sister. She'd never imagined he'd ever see her as a woman he desired.

It had taken almost half a year after he'd told her how his feelings for her had changed for her to stop marveling that they were in a relationship. She kept thinking about his track record with women and expecting things to go south. She wished she'd been surprised when things became strained.

Maybe they never should've taken the step from friends to romantically involved. It made her heart ache to think this way, but their inability to connect and work out their problems these last few months demonstrated that they'd rushed into a relationship that neither one was ready for. Could it be that Kyle felt the same way? Was he grappling with the same doubts she had?

Melody searched his expression, unable to discern what was going on in his mind. She thought back to the party, and how she'd tried to assuage everyone's curiosity and concern when she and Kyle left. At this point, aside from Dylan and Kyle, they all knew her secret. A feeling of dread slid down her spine. This wasn't going to be easy.

About three months into the tour with Nate's band Free Fall, Melody had begun to worry that the explosion of desire that had sustained her and Kyle through the beginning months of their relationship wasn't a solid foundation to build a future on. They'd only been a couple for nine months when she'd left LA to open for the award-winning pop band. Weeks and weeks on the road, with only occasional long weekends back in LA, had created an unsettling disassociation between her and Kyle that text messages and Skype calls hadn't been able to bridge.

Maybe if her track record with men had been more extensive she'd have had more confidence in her ability to keep Kyle's interest from thousands of miles away. From an early age she'd thrown herself into music rather than boys. Sure, she'd dated, but until Kyle came along, the guys she attracted were mostly like Hunter and way too much like her father: selfish and neglectful.

And then there was the fact that before her, Kyle's longest relationship had lasted four months. As a former pro baseball player, he had a pretty high profile lifestyle that women flocked to. Kyle was one hell of a catch and Melody recognized that every woman he met could be hotter and more famous than the last. So, she'd enjoyed their time together, never really expecting that it would last.

Before she'd realized it, they'd made it six months and he'd asked her to move in. Trent had been concerned when he'd learned about this escalation in their romance. He'd been Kyle's best friend for fifteen years and recognized that his friend was in deeper than he'd ever been before. Despite her brother's advice to slow down, Melody had taken the plunge and moved into Kyle's Hollywood Hills home.

Kyle's voice broke into her thoughts. "Why have you been avoiding me since the tour ended?"

"I've had a lot to think about," she said.

"Like what?"

Before they'd started dating, Melody had only ever seen Kyle as funny, sexy and supportive. He never demonstrated fear or anxiety or displayed a hint of vulnerability. His father had done a number on his psyche when Kyle was a young child, demanding his son stay in control of his emotions at all times. So it came as no great surprise that Kyle's first reaction to any little problem in their relationship was to shut down.

And yet, she'd been the one who'd taken a huge step back after his first big show of emotion. When he'd asked if she was cheating on him with Hunter, he'd been angry and hurt. His strong reaction to the paparazzi photo had caused her own emotions to flare.

Growing up the daughter of Siggy Caldwell hadn't allowed her to develop an understanding of healthy relationships. Her father was a hard man to like, much less love. Misogynistic, arrogant and selfish, he'd alienated his wives and his children with his disrespect.

So many times her father had declared he loved her right before launching into criticism, invalidating the claim while impressing on her that she was unworthy of his—or anyone else's—love.

While Kyle was nothing like her father, his accusation had awakened the same feelings of injustice she'd suffered as a little girl. As she'd done with her father, she'd shut Kyle out and walked away.

But that hadn't stopped her from loving him.

When she didn't answer him right away, Kyle spoke again. "Like what? Hunter?"

"No." She gave her head a vehement shake and followed it up with a weary sigh.

"Are you back in love with him?"

"No!" She stared at him in frustration. "Would you please let that go. I want to be with you."

His expression grew stonier. "You sure haven't been acting that way these last few months."

"It's not the same between us as before I went on the tour," she blurted out.

"I agree."

"Maybe if we go back and figure out where we went wrong," she said. "Or start over."

Was that even possible given the secret she was keeping from him?

"And if we can't?"

She didn't answer and their conversation didn't resume.

As Kyle drove into the gated community where Trent had his house, Melody wished she had some idea what he was thinking about. Her stomach was in knots. She pressed her sweaty palms against her coat and took deep, calming breaths, hoping to coax her confidence out of hiding.

Her nerves weren't under control by the time Kyle pulled into Trent's driveway and stopped the car. She had her door open and feet on the pavement before the

silence could get any more awkward. He was seconds
behind her as she keyed in the four-digit code that
opened the side gate leading to the backyard.

A paving-stone walkway led to her front door. Melody fumbled with her keys until Kyle pulled the ring
from her clumsy fingers and slid the correct one home.
His body brushed hers, awakening her longing to be
held in his arms, and she was a split second from
throwing herself against his chest when he took a deliberate step away from her.

"After you."

Melody bit back a miserable groan. "Thanks."

Knowing it would be dark when she returned, Melody had left the lights burning in the living room. The
heavy scent of roses hit her as soon as she entered. An
enormous bouquet of fat red blooms occupied the center of her dining table. The arrangement had appeared
at the studio the prior afternoon. She'd been thrilled
as she'd read the accompanying card.

I'm thankful for you.

There'd been no signature and Melody hadn't recognized the handwriting. This hadn't surprised her. She
suspected the order had been phoned in and the florist
had written the message. But when she'd studied the
card and the roses, she wasn't sure Kyle had sent them.

And now, as he helped Melody out of her coat, Kyle
didn't seem to notice the flowers. Which left her wondering if Hunter had sent them. If so, that was going
to complicate things between her and Kyle.

"Do you want something to drink?" She indicated

the kitchen, but Kyle didn't spare it a glance as he shook his head.

He seemed glued to the floor in the space between her living and dining rooms. Melody wondered what it would take to get him to sit down.

"Who are those from?" Kyle had at last noticed the roses.

"I'd hoped they were from you."

"I didn't send them." If Kyle noticed her rueful tone, he gave no indication. He moved toward the table. "Wasn't there a card?"

"Yes, but it wasn't signed."

"Are they from Hunter?"

"Sending me roses was never his style."

"Things change." His lips tightened. "Did you call and ask him?"

"No."

Melody had left the card on the table beside the crystal vase. Kyle picked it up and read the message.

"'I'm thankful for you'?" He shot her a frown. "What does that mean?"

Irritation rose at his sharp tone. She thought it was pretty obvious. "It's Thanksgiving. Maybe someone thought it was a timely message."

"Someone?"

"I don't know where the roses came from," she snapped, wishing Kyle would stop talking about the stupid flowers. She needed to tell him that she was pregnant, but had lost control of the conversation.

"You're sure?" He reread the card. "This seems awfully personal for it to have been written by a stranger.

Did you ask Trent or Savannah if they sent the flowers?"

"Yes. They didn't send them."

"Red roses are a romantic gesture," Kyle murmured to himself, tapping the card against his knuckles. He frowned at the plump red buds. "It seems like something a man in love would send."

Which was why she'd wished Kyle had sent them. Of course, despite being together for nine months and the fact that he'd invited her to move in with him, Kyle had never actually come out and said he loved her. He'd always been a cool customer when it came to women. The one who decided when it started and when it ended.

It was this tendency that had made her hesitate before choosing him over Hunter. She'd been worried about stepping from one relationship where she didn't feel safe and secure into another similar situation. Even so, in the end she'd following her instincts and taken a leap of faith. And despite their current problems, she still wouldn't say she'd been wrong.

"Why didn't you call Hunter and ask him?" Kyle asked, watching her through narrowed eyes as if waiting for her to slip up.

A thousand times in the last five months she'd regretted hanging out with Hunter in that New York City nightclub and then leaving at the same time he had. The whole thing had been innocent enough. There had been a crush of people outside the club and he'd grabbed her hand to avoid being separated as they'd run to the limo that had been waiting at the curb. Unfortunately, the media was obsessed with Hunter's love life and had blown up the incident, speculating that Hunter and Melody had reunited.

"Can you please forget about Hunter for two seconds." Melody didn't want Kyle's thoughts taking him there.

Since she'd run into Hunter in New York, Kyle had mentioned several times that she might have unfinished business with the DJ. That couldn't be farther from the case, but there were things she'd had in common with Hunter, like them both being in the music business, that she didn't share with Kyle.

Melody set her hand on his arm to bring his attention to her. "I have something I need to tell you."

When his hazel eyes shifted her way, she released the breath she'd been holding. It was long past time she got this off her chest, but now that the time had come, saying the words out loud was way harder than any speech she'd prepared in her head.

"Earlier I said things are complicated."

Cool eyes watched her from a face made of granite and Melody longed to be anywhere but here. Given Kyle's family background, he wasn't exactly emotive. He played his cards close to his chest. She had absolutely no idea how he was going to react to what she had to say. She could only hope the anticipation was worse than the outcome.

"I'm pregnant."

Kyle's flat expression vanished. Instead, he looked like the floor had dropped from beneath his feet. "Pregnant?"

"Yes. I know it's a shock…"

They hadn't anticipated this. The topic had never even come up. Nor had marriage or anything having to do with the future. Their relationship had been new and untested. They'd both committed to taking things one day at a time.

"You're having a baby." His gaze went past her shoulder and roved around the room as if he was in search of something to help him understand. Like a lodestone, the vase of red roses snagged his notice once more. His body went rigid. "And the father?"

Melody shook her head and took a step back. Had she heard him right? "What do you mean?"

"The father." Kyle flung out his hand in the direction of the flowers as if they explained everything. "Do you know who it is?"

Two

At his question, Melody blinked several times in rapid succession and then just stared at him in shock. As the impact of what he'd asked sunk in, Kyle realized he'd just made a huge mistake. His heart clenched in misery. The last thing he wanted to do was hurt her, but that was all he seemed capable of these days.

"What I meant was…" he began, but she was having none of it.

"You're the father," Melody said, her voice raw with disappointment and anguish. "How could you think anything else?"

"The flowers." He slashed his gaze toward them, unable to face the judgment in Melody's eyes. "It's the exact thing Hunter sent you last year when he was trying to get you to reconsider picking me over him."

"Hunter and I are friends." Her stiff tone brooked no argument. "Nothing more."

"The same could've been said about us before we got together," he reminded her.

For several seconds she stared at him in silence as her chest rose and fell in response to the large quantity of air she was moving through her lungs. Her blue eyes were overly bright as she assessed him.

When at last she spoke, her words thudded like hammer blows on his psyche. "I can't believe you could think that I would cheat on you with Hunter or anyone else."

The urge to fold her into his arms flooded him, but so much resentment lay between them. He doubted she'd be open to any attempt on his part to touch her.

"I don't."

"Then why would you ask me something so ridiculous as whether I know who the father is?"

"It came out wrong." But it hadn't. In the back of his mind was that ever-present image of Melody and Hunter hand-in-hand.

"I don't think it did. You've been looking for an excuse to break up for months." Her voice was ragged and raw. "I'm not going to fight you any longer. We're done."

"What?" Although he'd been dreading this outcome for months now, Kyle wasn't prepared for the actual ending. His thoughts reeled. "Just like that?"

"You just accused me of being pregnant with some random guy's baby—"

"Not some random guy," he reminded her, hating

the words coming out of his mouth but unable to stop the flow. He needed to get his suspicions out in the open. That was the only way they could move forward. His tone was bleak as he finished. "Hunter's."

"I can't keep doing this." Melody stuck out her arm and pointed toward the door. "Go."

The numbness that had momentarily gripped him burned away in a rush. "Aren't you forgetting something?" He gazed toward her belly where, now that he knew what to look for, he detected the tiniest roundness. "That's my baby you're carrying."

Muscles bunched in her cheek as her arm fell back to her side. Her eyes were sapphire-hard as she demanded, "So, now you're sure?"

If he wanted to save their relationship, he had to get over the doubts clouding his judgment. He loved Melody and they were going to be a family. He'd won her away from Hunter once. He could do it again. And again. Whatever it took.

"Yes."

She crossed her arms over her chest, not giving an inch. "And I'm supposed to forget every terrible thing you thought about me and be glad you've finally decided to come around?"

"I made a mistake."

"You made a series of them." Abruptly, the fight drained out of her. "This isn't how I wanted things to go."

"What did you expect?" He took a half step toward her, intent on making some sort of a peace offering, but let his hand fall back to his side when she shook her head.

"I don't know." Her shoulders rounded with exhaustion. "I thought maybe it would magically fix things."

"We've had too much time apart."

"And that's my fault?"

Although she'd been the one who'd pulled away rather than stay and fight with him—for them—he'd meant it as an observation, not a criticism. Her distance these last few months had awakened a fear of losing her.

"I told you to go on the tour," he reminded her. "And if I had to do it all over again, I'd make the same decision. It was the right step for your career." And if he was honest with himself, he hadn't been ready for the level of commitment their relationship had reached.

It still boggled his mind how fast he'd gone from being her friend to inviting her to move in with him. Cohabiting with Melody had been the most natural thing in the world. It hadn't required any significant shift in his beliefs or habits. The transformation from bachelor to boyfriend had been seamless and rewarding. It wasn't until she left on the tour that he'd noticed disquieting thoughts creeping in.

"How far along are you?"

"Twelve weeks."

He did the math. The last time they'd been together. It had been a rocky weekend. "How long have you known?"

"Since shortly after I returned from Sydney."

"Six weeks." He rubbed his eyes while disappointment flowed through him. Why had it taken her so long to share such important news? Could it be that she was afraid of how he would react? And hadn't he just demonstrated that she'd been right?

Her vehemence caught him by surprise. "You don't get to do that." She pointed an accusatory finger at him.

"Do what?"

"Make me feel bad for not rushing to tell you that everything in your life was going to change."

She was so obviously afraid of what his reaction would be. And perhaps with good reason. He hadn't exactly swept her into his arms and spun her in a giddy circle while crowing his delight.

"I'm sorry."

"It's fine." But she appeared anything but okay. She seemed as shell-shocked as he was. "I'm sure we're both overwhelmed at the idea of becoming parents. At least we have six months to get used to the idea."

"Have you started to think about what you're going to do?" he asked.

"What do you mean 'do'?"

"For where you're going to live." Where did he figure in her plans? "Are you staying here?"

"In Las Vegas?" Melody looked like a cornered rabbit. "I don't know. Nate is here. And Mia. Trent, Savannah and Dylan will be coming back as soon as she's done filming the movie."

"It doesn't much sound like you plan on coming back to LA."

Or back to Kyle. His home was in LA. Although,

at the moment he was renting a place outside Vegas for the next few months. He'd offered to take over as temporary manager of Club T's for two reasons. To be closer to Melody while she finished her album and to free up Trent to live in LA and take care of his son while Savannah worked.

"I feel as if I have a really good support system here." The subtext was clear. She didn't think he was going to be there for her. Was this opinion recently acquired or something that had occurred to her over a period of time?

"How do you figure? Trent and Savannah are in LA at the moment."

"They'll be coming back as soon as Savannah is done with her movie. And you're here."

Something loosened in his chest. "So you do want me around."

"Of course. I want us to be a family." Nothing sounded better, but in his peripheral vision a dozen red roses stood like a stop sign on her dining room table.

Then she shook her head. "Is that possible? Can we get back to where we were before the tour?"

"I'm not sure we can." Although Kyle doubted it was the sort of answer a pregnant woman wanted to hear from the father of her child, he had to be honest with her. "Go backward, I mean. I'm sorry. All this has caught me by surprise. I never imagined myself a dad."

"We never talked about it. I was a bit afraid to, knowing how you and your father get along."

"You mean don't get along."

She gave a little shrug. "You aren't him. You're going to be a great dad."

He wanted some time to assimilate all he'd learned, but she was staring at him like she needed him to fix everything. He just had no idea how to begin.

He considered her remark about his relationship with his father.

Suck it up, kid.

Be a man.

No one's going to help you unless you help yourself.

The clichés went on and on. Maybe if Brent Tailor hadn't been such a successful businessman and dedicated philanthropist, his opinions would've been easier to ignore. Instead, he was someone Kyle looked up to professionally. And much of what his father drilled into him had enabled his success as a major league pitcher.

The downside to what his dad had drilled into him all his life was that it didn't enable Kyle to celebrate all he'd achieved in his baseball career or convey to Melody how he felt about their relationship.

"And you're going to be a great mother."

She blew out a huge breath. "I hope so. It would've been better if it happened later rather than sooner."

"What's done is done. What do you need from me?" He saw her answer coming and spoke quickly to head it off. "And don't say nothing."

From her frown he knew he'd struck the truth. She'd grown up watching her father and brother butt heads and depending on the situation, tended to either retreat or take on the role of peacekeeper whenever she caught a whiff of conflict.

"I have a doctor's appointment tomorrow." Her voice came across as tentative as if she half expected him to refuse.

"What time?"

"Three o'clock."

Excitement trickled into his awareness, diluting his dismay. She was pregnant with his child. It wasn't great timing, nor was becoming a father something he'd imagined happening any time soon, but he'd watched Trent with Dylan and was pretty sure he'd never seen his friend this happy. Maybe there was something to being a family that made the big problems smaller.

"Where do you want me to pick you up?" he asked.

"You don't need to come."

"Oh, I'm not missing this."

Trent and Savannah had overcome bigger obstacles to find their way back to each other. Surely Kyle and Melody could get past what stood between them. Of course, he was assuming she wanted to. What if she didn't love him anymore? She might not have cheated on him with Hunter, but he'd treated her as if she had.

He'd broken her trust, lodged unfair accusations at her. The person in the wrong hadn't been her, but him. Just that morning he'd been all set to forgive her. It had never occurred to Kyle that the one in need of pardoning would be him.

"Thank you," Melody said, but the words were perfunctory as if her thoughts had traveled elsewhere. "I appreciate your willingness to be involved."

"I'm going to be there for you every way I can."

Melody sat in the small, utilitarian lobby of Ugly Trout Records and stared out the front window toward the parking lot. For the fifth time in ten minutes, she checked the time on her phone. Kyle had three more minutes before he could be considered late. Since last night, she'd regretted caving in to his offer to take her to the doctor's appointment. Unlike Hunter, Kyle counted punctuality as one of his virtues. He'd never left her waiting and wondering if he was going to call or show up. He'd always been very clear about his intentions and then followed through.

So why was she working herself into such a frantic mess? Practicing patience, Melody smoothed her sweaty palms down the legs of her skinny jeans. Thank goodness the denim had some stretch to it. Thanks to the severity of her morning sickness these last few weeks, she'd lost weight, but today her baby bump seemed more pronounced than the week before.

This change—more than the pregnancy test, her constant nausea and fatigue—had made her all too aware that she had a baby inside her. Sweat broke out. Most days she was happy about her impending motherhood. The timing could be better. She was on the verge of dropping her first album and the stress wasn't good for her or the baby. But now that she'd broken the news to Kyle, more than just her and her baby's future weighed on her mind.

"Hey, Melody, what are you doing up here?"

She turned at the sound of her name and smiled at the man who was detouring toward her. Craig Jameson was one of the top sound engineers working at the label. He'd been involved in eighty percent of Melody's recording sessions and been instrumental in helping her produce most of her songs. He had a knack for knowing exactly what each song needed.

They'd spent hours together in the studio, talking about music and the industry. He had great stories about various artists that had come to Ugly Trout to record. Many had involved some pretty outrageous behavior—drunken jam sessions, a party with strippers and several fistfights.

"I'm waiting for Kyle to pick me up." Although her relationship with Kyle was pretty well-known around the studio thanks to their public personas, Craig knew more details due to all the time he and Melody had spent together.

"It's a little late for lunch."

"Actually, we are heading to…" She'd held off mentioning her pregnancy around the studio until she told Kyle, but now that he knew there was no reason to keep the secret any longer. "The doctor."

"You okay?" Craig's concern touched Melody.

"Fine. Actually more than fine." She forced bright happiness into her tone. "I'm pregnant."

"That's great news. Then things between you and Kyle are better?"

During a particularly low point, she'd confided in Craig. At the time she hadn't considered that Craig was a work colleague. A few days earlier, he'd told her that he'd just broken off with his girlfriend of a year. She hadn't hesitated to offer him a sympathetic shoulder. Maybe it had crossed a line, but Craig was a decent guy who'd needed a friend.

"We're working on it." She smiled, but there wasn't a lot of joy in it.

"He'd be a fool to let you go."

"That's sweet of you to say." Tears surged to her eyes but Melody blinked them away. It seemed as if everything set her off these days. Hormones. They were driving her crazy. She'd never been moody, but since becoming pregnant, her emotions were all over the place. "There's Kyle now. I should be back in an hour or so. Would you have some time later to sit down with me? Nate wants me to get my album done and I could use some help narrowing down the songs."

"I'd be honored to help."

"Let me know what time you're free." She headed toward the front door and paused with her hand on it. When she looked over her shoulder, Craig was still watching her. "And thanks."

"For what?"

"Everything." Feeling a little as if she'd said too much, Melody pushed the door and blinked in the bright sunlight.

Kyle had parked his car and was heading toward her along the front walk. His long legs ate up the distance between them, demonstrating his upbeat mood. Today he wore a pair of khaki slacks and navy V-neck sweater over a white button-down shirt. His thick brown hair had an artfully disheveled look she loved. With a long, square face, firm chin and well-shaped lips, Kyle had the sort of good looks favored by fashion designers looking for sexy, rugged models.

When Melody saw his unguarded smile, a weight lifted off her shoulders. For a second she was catapulted back in time to when they'd first been living together in LA. It had been a heady, exciting, romantic three months. Kyle had been super supportive of her career and interested in learning her process for writing music.

His fascination had drawn Melody out of her shell. When it came to songwriting, she'd learned to be exceptionally protective. Back when she was still in school, her father had belittled her talent and broken down her confidence. He'd wanted her to pursue classical violin and made her attend Juilliard. When she'd quit halfway through her third year, choosing instead to pursue the contemporary popular music she loved, Siggy had pretty much disowned her.

"You ready?" he asked as he neared.

It seemed the most natural thing in the world for him to wrap his arms around her and drop a kiss on her cheek. Although she longed for a proper kiss, the affection in the gesture sent warmth rushing through her.

"I'm ready," she countered. "Are you?"

Kyle's smile was ever so slightly crooked as he opened the passenger door and ushered her inside. "I am."

"I'm glad." She studied him as he walked around

the car and slid behind the wheel once more. "I'm a little nervous about the ultrasound."

"Why?" Kyle got the car started and pulled out of the parking lot before glancing her way. "I thought this was just routine."

"It is. But they look for certain things. I can't help but wonder what they might find."

"What are they going to look for?" Kyle's brow creased.

Melody instantly regretted sharing her concerns. The last thing she wanted to do was freak out Kyle. He'd only just learned about the baby and probably hadn't yet come to terms with becoming a father and now she was heaping new concerns onto the pile.

"They'll check the heartbeat and determine my due date."

"None of that sounds too bad."

"Nooo." She drew the word out. "And then they'll look to make sure everything looks normal. Two arms. Two legs. That the organs are developing okay." There were just so many things that could be wrong. And so many things that could be right. When had she become such a pessimist?

"Is there any reason to think anything will be missing?"

His faint note of teasing as he asked the question lightened Melody's mood. She was being anxious for no good reason.

"Of course not. I guess it's just going to be more real after today."

And Kyle would be beside her as they both saw their

baby for the first time. It roused all the things she so badly wanted but was afraid she might never get. For the last several weeks, since she'd learned she was pregnant, she'd been so focused on what was wrong with their relationship that she hadn't thought about all the things that had once been right.

She'd braced herself to be a single mom, not even giving Kyle the benefit of the doubt. Because of the way her father had often treated her, she'd been quick to expect Kyle to disappoint her. If she anticipated Kyle not wanting to be a father, then it wouldn't hurt as much when that was what happened.

Automatically going on the defensive certainly wasn't fair to Kyle. Or herself. Or their baby.

"There's no going back," she said.

He shot her a curious look. "Do you want to go back?"

"You didn't ask for this."

"Did you?"

"You mean did I try to get pregnant?" Melody wasn't sure how to take his question.

"I wasn't asking if you deliberately became pregnant," he said and then sighed. He reached for her hand. "I was merely reflecting your question back at you."

His matter-of-fact reaction to their situation should be the perfect balm for her agitation, but for some reason she was finding his encouragement annoying. At the same time, his fingers gave a little squeeze and she found herself torn between wanting to fight with him and needing to give in to his attempt to connect with her.

"If I've learned anything in the last year it's that it's really hard to maintain relationships while on the road. I thought a lot about what would happen if I decide to take my career seriously. I'd be traveling a lot on tour and making appearances. That sort of life is hard on everyone."

"And you're worried that you can't have your career and a baby." He didn't voice the obvious question: whether she'd intended to choose between her career and continuing her relationship with him. "I think you can do it all." A pause. "If you want to."

This was the decision she was dreading. Did she want it all? A family? A career? Her feelings for Kyle hadn't changed, but things were so much more complicated these days.

"Do you want to give us another shot?" she asked, her heart thudding hard against her ribs.

"I think we owe it to ourselves to do so, don't you?"

"I do."

He didn't seem all that happy with her answer, however. "Just tell me one thing. Would you have been willing to work things out if you weren't pregnant?"

"Yes, because if I didn't, there would always be something unfinished hanging between us."

He waited a long time before answering. "That's fair. But you should probably know I wanted you back before I knew you were pregnant."

"Even though you didn't trust me?"

And there was the crux of their whole problem.

"I was wrong to think you and Hunter got together."

She could tell that declaration had required a great deal of effort, but it wasn't enough. "And yet last night you were wondering if I knew which of you was the father of my baby."

Three

Kyle knew he deserved her sarcasm and let it slide off rather than get defensive. "It was the roses and that weird card that threw me off."

"It was pretty weird, but it was probably just a screwup on the florist's part. Maybe they neglected to add the person's signature to the card. It could be from any number of people."

"You don't think it's unusual that someone sent you a dozen red roses?" The last thing he should be doing was arguing with her.

"Okay, it's freaking me out that I don't know who sent them. But it was a nice gesture."

Melody might not think the roses came from Hunter, but Kyle was pretty sure he'd sent them.

"Can we forget about the flowers?" Melody continued, smoothing her hands over her knees. "I want to focus on this appointment. I'm really glad you came along today."

"So am I." But even as he spoke, Kyle recognized it was going to take more than accompanying her to a doctor's appointment before the tension eased between them.

He would have to make an effort to put his doubts to rest and get back in Melody's good graces. If that required romantic gestures like flowers and candlelit dinners, he would do whatever it took.

"You can take a right at the driveway coming up." Melody pointed the way into a parking lot beside a plain five-story building.

"You've been here before?"

"A couple times."

"So, you are planning to have the baby in Las Vegas."

Melody's mouth opened, but no words came out. She bit her lip and stared down at her hands. "It makes sense."

"But your life is in LA. With me." Or at least it had been before she'd gone on tour.

"We haven't really lived together these last nine months," she said.

"When I encouraged you to go on the tour, I thought you'd be coming back. All your stuff is still in my house."

"I just need a little time."

"How much time?"

"I don't know."

Kyle parked the car before responding. "I don't like living in limbo."

"Then maybe we should break up."

This wasn't at all what he expected her to say. "Where is this coming from?"

"I just don't know where we stand anymore. We're not dating. We're not living together. Are we even still friends?"

Her bald statement of the facts as she saw them swept his feet out from under him. It was as if his world had tilted and his head connected with the pavement. His thoughts grew foggy and indistinct.

"My feelings for you haven't changed."

"You can't seriously believe that's true." Melody opened her car door and slipped out, leaving Kyle staring at nothing.

She was halfway to the building before he roused himself and chased after her. "Okay," he said as he caught up with her. "Maybe we're not in the same place as we were before you left on the tour, but that doesn't mean I'm done. I want you in my life. I want to be there for our baby. How do you see your future?"

"Honestly, I sort of go back and forth between wanting us to be a happy family and thinking it might be better if I raise this baby on my own."

"That's not going to happen." His father hadn't been there for him. Kyle intended for his child to have a loving, attentive father.

"Because it hurts when I think how much I love you and wonder if you'll ever feel the same about me." They stopped before the elevator and she gave him a long searching look. "I'm afraid to have my heart broken."

Kyle wished he could tell her he'd never hurt her, but he already had when he'd assumed she'd hooked up with Hunter that night in New York City. And again just yesterday when he jumped to the wrong conclusion about the baby's paternity. Why couldn't he just put his faith in her and in their relationship?

Because he didn't know how.

His parents hadn't given him the emotional tools to be successful in a romantic partnership. His father had ruthlessly controlled all feelings good and bad, preferring to navigate through life's up and downs with logic. Kyle's mother on the other hand was a fearful, anxious woman who loved her son almost too much. Trapped between an emotional storm and an impassive granite wall, Kyle had stopped expressing how he felt and let everyone think he was okay all the time.

His teammates in school and then in the major leagues called him the Iceman because he was always chill. But it was a mask, not a true representation of how he felt. No matter how relaxed and unaffected he looked, inside he seethed with doubt, desire and sometimes disappointment.

But thanks to his father's tutelage, Kyle's first reaction to everything life threw at him was to slide on his aviator sunglasses and summon an enigmatic smile. No matter what the stakes, how bad the loss or how well he pitched, he was the Iceman. Even after his first no-hitter, he'd given only a sly smile to the mass of reporters who'd come to interview him in the aftermath.

"I don't want to hurt you," Kyle said and meant it, but he knew he didn't always behave the way she needed him to.

Sometimes it was as if what made him so happy in their relationship was the exact thing that caused him to regress back to the self-protective behaviors he learned in childhood. He retreated from strong emotion instead of owning it. These last few months since he'd thought he lost her to Hunter had been some of the worst of his life.

Instead of reaching out and telling her how afraid he was to lose her, he'd shoved down his fears and made it seem as if he was okay. But he wasn't okay. In fact, he was a mess, which was why he'd jumped to the wrong conclusion about her feelings for Hunter.

While Melody checked in with the receptionist, Kyle glanced around the waiting area, seeing women in various stages of pregnancy. This was really happening. He was going to be a father. Time to step up and take care of the mother of his child. Whatever that meant.

"I think we should get married," he said as she took a seat beside him.

Her eyes widened. "You're kidding, right?"

"Not at all. It makes sense. I don't want to be a part-time father and we are good together."

"Good together?" She looked at him as if he'd sprouted a second head. "We've barely spoken to each other these last few months. Neither one of us is very good at communicating how we feel." Like Kyle had, she regarded the other expectant mothers in their various stages of pregnancy. "I don't think we're ready for marriage."

Although her answer frustrated him, Kyle reminded himself that it wasn't always going to be like this between them. He would find a way to make things all right again.

"So we work on our communication," he said, hoping she grasped how determined he was to make things work.

"How are we going to do that?"

"We'll go see a couples counselor. Someone who can teach us how to express ourselves in a positive way."

Her stiff posture highlighted her discomfort. "I don't know."

"Look," he said. "We might have been able to walk away months ago, but things have changed. And I'd like to point out that while we've hit a rough patch, I don't see either one of us calling it quits." He chose to ignore that not ten minutes earlier she'd suggested they break up.

"I agree we should make an effort to be friends again for the sake of the baby." She looked flustered and unsure what she planned to say next. "But marriage is a huge leap."

"Let's table that for now." Now that he'd suggested they marry, he was convinced it was the best idea. He didn't want to be his child's part-time father. "We'll have dinner tonight and talk about it."

She shifted on the cushioned chair as if it was made of hard plastic. "I can't tonight. I'm working late. Nate has given me until the fifth of December to finish my album."

"Good for him. You've been working on it on and off for a year. I know you're a perfectionist, but at some point you have to let it go."

And maybe then he'd be able to refocus some of her attention on their struggling relationship. He knew her music was important to her, but there had to be a way for her to be a success in her career and still have room for her personal life.

"I know, but it's my first album and I want everything to be the best it can."

He understood her quest for perfection. As a teenager he'd spent hours learning how to place a pitch over the center of the plate. The familiar repetition of wind up and throw allowed him to forget his troubles and focus on the here and now. Watching Melody get lost in her songwriting process, he'd recognized the same need to make something flawless and beautiful.

"And yet you won't know how good it is," he said, reaching for her hand, offering her both support and encouragement, "until you put it out there."

She squeezed his fingers and gave a little laugh. "Or how much people are going to hate it."

"Stop channeling your father. If the man knew good talent when he heard it, he wouldn't have run his label into the ground."

"You're right, but it's hard to ignore all the times he told me to stick with the violin because I didn't have what it took to be a songwriter or a singer."

Kyle wondered what it would take for her to believe

she deserved to be successful. He'd tried to reassure her, but often felt as if she couldn't accept his uplifting words because he didn't have any musical cred.

"And yet you've proved him wrong so many times," he reminded her. "This album is going to do great. You'll see."

"You've always supported me and I really appreciate it."

The warmth in her eyes aroused a pang of longing so acute he almost couldn't breathe. Damn. He missed her.

"Melody?" A blonde woman in pale blue scrubs appeared in the doorway.

Melody practically sprang to her feet and shot him a worried look. "Are you ready for this?"

Kyle gave her a reassuring smile as he tucked her hand into the crook of his arm. "Absolutely."

Melody followed the nurse into the patient room. Kyle's broad shoulders and strong presence filled the small space. He sat beside her in attentive silence while the nurse took her blood pressure, frowning over its elevated status, and asked routine questions. She answered automatically, trying to ignore the doubts that flickered on the edge of her awareness brought on by his shocking proposal.

What was he thinking to ask her to marry him without forethought or fanfare? Not that she needed a whole huge production made out of getting engaged, but it would've been nice to be proposed to in a romantic setting by a man who adored her instead of in a clinical setting by a man who just learned the day before that he was going to be a father.

I think we should get married.

His blunt declaration had been more practical suggestion than impassioned plea. Once the shock faded, her first impulse had been to hit him. How dare he presume she would agree to marry him because she was pregnant? And then tears had threatened and she'd had to grip the edge of her chair to keep from bawling her eyes out in reception.

"Your blood pressure is a little high," the nurse said, glancing at her with a thoughtful look.

"I'm nervous about the ultrasound," she lied. It was the conversation with Kyle that had upset her.

He might not have told her he loved her, but she knew that he was committed to her and their baby. Whether that meant they would find their way back to being happy with each other was the big question.

"That's not unusual, but we should check it again before you leave."

The nurse finished adding Melody's data into the computer and then showed her the gown she needed to don for the ultrasound. Kyle's stoic expression gave away none of his thoughts as he watched the nurse exit the room.

"Close your eyes," Melody told him as she began to work the buttons free on her shirt. She was already feeling vulnerable enough without adding to her stress by stripping in front of him.

One corner of his lips rose in that sexy half smile that made butterflies erupt in her stomach. "I've seen you naked before." His heavy-lidded gaze slid over her body, cataloging her curves with deliberate possessiveness.

Melody ignored the ache that flared between her thighs. Over these last few months, she'd deluded herself into thinking she was a practical woman who didn't need a man. She was perfectly capable of making rational decisions about her future and sticking to them.

Yet, a single flirtatious grin from Kyle swiftly showed her how erroneous her assumptions had been. She actually took a half step in his direction, intent on cupping his strong face in her palms and sliding her open mouth against his in a sizzling kiss.

"Just do it," she told him, wrenching her wayward hormones back under control.

Without saying another word he let his lashes drift downward, but the smile didn't drift from his lips. For a moment she stared at his familiar features with such longing she thought she might start to cry. Her hands shook as she slipped off her low boots and set them beneath her chair. Despite being confident he wouldn't peek, Melody quickly stripped down and put on the front-closing gown.

"Okay," she said, paper crinkling beneath her as she sat on the exam table.

"How about Amelia if it's a girl?" Kyle's voice was heavy with intent. "Austin if it's a boy."

She couldn't stop the grin that twitched on her lips. "You've been thinking about baby names?"

"I didn't sleep very well last night." He pulled out

his phone and stared at the screen. "I'm also fond of Aubrey and Addison."

"Did you get out of the A's?"

He scrolled down some sort of list on his phone. "Colton for a boy?"

Her throat locked up as she stared at him. Damn the man for driving her crazy with his unromantic proposal of marriage and then twisting her heart into knots with this sweet demonstration of how excited he was to be a dad. Before she could respond, the door opened and the doctor appeared.

"How are you doing today?" Dr. Sara Evans asked, advancing into the room and taking quick stock of Melody's state of mind before glancing toward Kyle, who'd gotten to his feet. "And you are?"

"Kyle Tailor, the father."

Dr. Evans gave a quick nod before getting started. Almost as soon as her doctor had entered the room, Melody had calmed down. She liked the obstetrician's keen gaze and brisk manner.

"I'm going to spread a little gel here." The doctor applied the clear goo to her belly and chuckled as Melody shivered. "It's a little bit chilly. You'll forget all about that in a second."

Melody stared down at the slight bump just below her belly button where her baby lay. When she glanced toward Kyle, she noticed his eyes were glued to the monitor where an image had begun to develop. And there it was. Their baby. Head. Arms. Legs. A whole little person inside her.

While both she and Kyle had been gaping at the

screen, Dr. Evans prattled on about the development of the fetus and the fact that the organs were developing.

"About this time," Dr. Evans said, "your baby will begin to open and close his or her fingers and his or her mouth will begin making sucking movements. He—or she—is about the size of a lime. Do you want to know the sex?"

Kyle spoke up before Melody could even open her mouth. "Can we?" His eyes sought hers. "Do you want to?"

"I guess." In truth she hadn't really thought about it. Didn't the pregnancy have to be further along? "Sure."

It would make planning easier if she knew she was having a boy or girl. She'd have to get the nursery ready and buy clothes. Of course, this brought up something that Kyle kept asking her about. Where was she going to live? She'd given up her apartment in LA to move in with Kyle. Trent's guest cottage was for guests. Up until now, she'd stayed for a couple days or a long weekend here and there when she took a break from the tour to work on her album.

She could justify living there while Trent was in LA with Savannah and Dylan, and she'd considered what would happen when they came back. They were family now. They would want their privacy.

When Kyle had asked her where she planned to live, she'd frozen up. With everything that was going on with her album and telling Kyle that she was pregnant, she'd been taking things one day at a time. Today, staring at the image of her baby on the monitor, decisions she had yet to make rushed at her.

Pressure on her fingers brought her back to the present. She winced a little at the bite of Kyle's grip, but his eyes were glued to the screen and he didn't seem to notice the way he was holding her hand. She squeezed back, bringing his focus to her.

"Looks like you're having a girl," Dr. Evans announced brightly, her smile broad. "Congratulations."

Melody was numb. "Are you sure?"

Dr. Evans nodded. "No question. This little girl isn't one bit shy."

"Then she'll take after her father," Melody murmured.

Her head spun. A girl. She glanced at Kyle to see his reaction, half expecting his expression to reflect disappointment. Had he imagined himself teaching his son to pitch? Instead, he was staring at her stomach and looking dazed. And delighted.

She waited until Dr. Evans finished with the ultrasound and left the room before she voiced the concern burning a hole in her stomach.

"You're okay with a girl?"

"Of course." He blinked several times and seemed to have trouble focusing on her. A line appeared between his brows. "Why would you think it wouldn't be?"

"Because you're a guy, you love baseball. I bet you woke up this morning thinking you needed to run out and buy a mitt and a ball."

"Actually, I woke up this morning thinking how empty my bed was without you in it."

She hadn't expected this angle of attack and wasn't

prepared with an evasive maneuver. Holding the gown closed as best she could, she sat up and spun so that her feet dangled. "Close your eyes. I need to get dressed."

Kyle braced his hands on the exam bed and leaned forward so he could peer directly into her eyes. "We're having a girl."

Placing her hand on his cheek, she whispered, "We are."

His grin was infectious and she found herself smiling back. He was close enough that all she had to do was lean forward a few inches to bring their lips into contact. He covered her fingers with his. The connection made her heart race. It would be so easy to just forget how hurt she'd been these last few months. Through passion and desire, they could start again. She didn't really need to return to the studio today. Instead, they could go to his house and make love all afternoon. Her toes curled at the thought.

She gathered breath and summoned her courage to suggest they do that, but the opportunity was lost when his phone began to ring. He pulled it out and frowned at the screen.

"It's the club. I need to get this. How about I meet you in the lobby."

"Sure." With a sigh, Melody watched him go, and then got dressed once more.

It was for the best, she decided. Part of the reason they were in this mess was because they'd rushed in before determining if they were really compatible. They'd been dating for too short a period of time before she'd moved in and the decision had been made out of convenience rather than a thoughtful evaluation of whether they could work as a couple.

And why was that? Because Melody had been afraid to put the brakes on. To ask the questions that might drive Kyle away. Now she realized that had been a mistake. And no matter how hard it might be to keep from falling back under Kyle's spell, until she knew for sure that he truly loved her, she couldn't move forward with their relationship.

Four

Kyle caught himself grinning as he negotiated the Las Vegas traffic on his way to Ugly Trout Records. The entire afternoon, since finding out they were having a girl, he'd been floating in a bubble of optimism. Now that the initial shock of his impending fatherhood had faded, he was feeling as if everything that had gone wrong with his and Melody's relationship was just a series of misunderstandings that they could sort out with a little work. They were going to be parents. Their daughter deserved to grow up in a secure, loving environment and he intended to provide that for her whatever it took.

Which was why he'd decided to start his campaign by bringing dinner to Melody at the recording studio so she could see he intended to take care of her. On the passenger seat sat a bag filled with several items that topped Melody's favorites list. It would have been better if they'd been in LA and he could've gone to Mama Rosa's for the Bucatini Alla Carbonara, but he thought what he'd found would pass muster.

He'd also discovered a place that made the most fantastic cheesecakes. He'd brought a sampler for her to gorge on. She'd lost weight these last few months and he couldn't imagine that was good for the baby.

Ever since seeing that tiny profile and hearing that his daughter was now moving her fingers and toes, he'd been filled with optimism. He was going to be a dad. The thought held nothing but joy. Sure, he had no idea what he was doing, but that didn't mean he couldn't learn. After all, he'd seen the way Trent had taken to being Dylan's father.

Trent, who'd sworn all his days that he'd never get married and have kids. His best friend had grown up with a terrible role model for fatherhood. Siggy Caldwell's ruthless tyranny in business carried over into his personal life. He had picked favorites among his children, choosing to lavish praise on his firstborn while criticizing both Trent and Melody. No matter how successful they were, neither one could do anything right in Siggy's opinion.

And yet both of his younger children managed to become affectionate, caring people. In Trent's case it had taken becoming a father and admitting he was in love with Savannah before his true nature emerged.

Melody hadn't learned to guard her emotions the way her brother had. She was more inclined to throw herself into a relationship with little regard for her self-esteem. That was how she'd been with Hunter. While she'd been dating the DJ, it had driven Kyle crazy to see her always making excuses for the way Hunter treated her. And yet that was not how she'd reacted when faced with problems in her relationship with Kyle.

Instead of laughing off his assumptions about her and Hunter, she'd been furious and they'd had a terrible fight. He couldn't remember her ever arguing with Hunter. Was that because her feelings for the DJ had been deeper and more profound? If so, why had she chosen Kyle in the end?

The driveway leading into the record label's parking lot appeared just ahead of him. He couldn't wait to see the look on Melody's face when he surprised her with dinner. She loved it when he was spontaneous.

Grabbing a parking space near the front entrance, he exited the car. It was close to six o'clock, and the lot was half full. Nate made the studio available twenty-four hours. The rate for off-peak hours was significantly cheaper, which made recording sessions affordable for up-and-coming artists. Melody took advantage of the quieter evenings to work on her album.

Kyle was reaching for the glass front door when he spied two people approaching through the lobby. His chest tightened as he recognized Hunter's tall form alongside Melody's slim figure. They were engaged in an animated conversation and hadn't yet spied him. He yanked open the glass door with more force than necessary.

"Kyle." Melody's eyes widened as she noticed him entering the building. "What are you doing here?"

He held up the bag. "I brought you dinner. I thought you'd be working."

His gaze flicked to Hunter. The DJ's lack of concern caused Kyle's annoyance to spike. Why was Melody leaving with him?

"Oh that's so…nice." She glanced at Hunter. Was it guilt that flickered in her eyes? "We were just going to grab something."

"And now you don't have to." Kyle pushed down his irritation and smiled. "I brought all your favorites. I thought you could show me what you've been working on while we eat."

When Melody hesitated, Kyle's gut twisted. He must not argue with her. Not today. Not after what they'd shared at the doctor's office. Seeing their baby for the first time had brought them closer than they'd been in months. He would not ruin that new beginning because he was annoyed that she was heading out to have dinner with Hunter.

"Sure. You don't mind?" she asked Hunter.

"It's fine." Hunter took in Kyle's tense expression before flashing a knowing smile. "You kids go have fun. I'll catch up with you later."

Kyle didn't bother to watch him go before catching Melody's elbow and turning her in the direction of the hallway that led to the various recording studios. He could feel a trace of resistance and noticed her glance over her shoulder in Hunter's direction. He tried not to let it bother him, but something about seeing Melody with Hunter made it hard for him to be rational.

"So were you two working on something together?" He thought the question came out sounding neutral enough.

"No, I was working with Craig when Hunter stopped by to ask me to dinner. I didn't even realize I was hungry until he mentioned grabbing a burger."

They entered a control booth. She snagged a couple bottles of water out of the mini-fridge, and then sat on the couch and watched while Kyle unpacked the food onto the coffee table.

"I brought pasta, salad and a cheesecake for dessert." He eyed her to gauge her reaction. She didn't seem overly thrilled by any of his choices. "I didn't realize you were eating red meat these days," he added, wondering what else about her he didn't know.

"It's being pregnant, I think. I've been craving all kinds of weird things. And there's some stuff I can't stand the smell of anymore."

"I hope shrimp isn't one of them because I brought you lemon Parmesan garlic shrimp over angel hair pasta."

"No, shrimp is fine. It's weird but I can't stand the smell of peanut butter." She popped the top off the plastic container and rolled her eyes in pleasure as the sent wafted from the bowl. "I ordered a salad with Thai peanut sauce a few weeks ago and it sent me scrambling for the bathroom."

"But you love peanut butter." They'd once taken

a jar to bed and enjoyed licking the sticky stuff off each other.

"And hopefully I will again once the baby comes." She shuddered. "In the meantime I'm staying far away." Her eyes widened when he brought out dessert. "Whoa, is that cheesecake?"

He nodded. "I brought you several kinds to choose from. Or you can eat them all."

"You went to a lot of trouble," she said, giving him a soft smile that made his pulse race and his mouth go dry.

"It's not any trouble taking care of you. And that's my plan from now on. You and the baby are my top priority."

"That sounds really great." Suddenly there were tears in her eyes. She laughed as she dashed them away. "I swear everything makes me cry these days."

"Not everything, I hope."

"Mostly when people are nice to me."

"Then you must be crying a lot because you're someone people want to be nice to."

Melody stopped eating and stared at him. "That's really sweet of you to say."

"I wasn't trying to be sweet," Kyle said. "I was just stating a fact."

"What time are you heading to the club?"

"I plan to get there around nine." He surveyed her features, gauging the level of her exhaustion. "How late are you planning on staying here? You look like you could use some rest."

As if on cue, she yawned. "I thought to stick around

for another couple hours. Hunter offered to help me with the bridge for one of my songs."

"Do you think it's a good idea that you're working with him?" The question slipped out before he could stop it.

"I don't understand what you mean." She frowned at him.

"He still has feelings for you. Why else would he have taken a job at Club T's and come to Ugly Trout to work with his clients?"

"Because Trent offered him a ridiculous amount of money to DJ?" Her blue eyes glittered as she regarded him. "And me being here isn't why he is using the facilities."

"He could just as easily record in LA." And oh how Kyle wished he would. "I'm sure most of his artists would prefer that."

"Hunter likes the vibe at Ugly Trout. And you know how fantastic Nate is to work with. I'm sure he's hoping to do a little collaborating with him."

Kyle stared at his penne in spicy vodka tomato cream sauce and found his appetite had vanished. Somehow this delightful surprise for Melody had led to a disagreeable revelation for him.

"You really need to get over this antagonism you have toward Hunter."

"I'll get over it when you convince me he doesn't want you back." And when she convinced him that she was going to stop running from their problems.

"He doesn't. In fact, he's been seeing Ivy Bliss."

"I thought he was just producing her new album."

The pop princess had been recording her latest album with Nate at Ugly Trout Records up until a couple weeks ago when artistic differences caused Ivy to walk away.

"Apparently they've been involved professionally and personally. So you can see there's no reason for you to worry."

Kyle nodded. Upsetting Melody with his suspicions was only going to drive her further away. The smart thing to do would be to figure out a different way to get the DJ to back off. Except that Hunter wasn't the whole problem.

"There's just one last thing that's been on my mind," he said in careful tones. The question that had been eating at him for a long time could no longer be contained.

"What?"

"When things started to go wrong. First between you and Hunter and later between us." His heart thundered as her full attention became locked on him. "Why did you fight for Hunter and run away from me?"

At Kyle's question, Melody found herself opening and closing her mouth like a fish out of water. Her brain seized like an overtaxed computer. He was right. She had done that and it wasn't at all fair. She couldn't explain why for a year and a half she'd put up with Hunter taking her for granted, but when Kyle challenged her on one thing—granted it was a pretty huge thing—she'd shut him down the same way she had…her father.

"It was different with Hunter." Immediately she saw this was the wrong thing to say. She shouldn't compare the two relationships. Yet how else to explain? "He neglected me. I was always chasing after him, never quite knowing if he wanted me or not."

"And I never did any of those things. You know I want you in my life."

She gave a reluctant nod, unsure how to explain herself. Maybe it was that her relationship with Kyle felt more important than what she'd had with Hunter.

"You hurt me."

Kyle's eyes widened. "How many times did Hunter make you cry?"

"Dozens."

The media had linked him with several women while he'd been seeing Melody. Hunter had claimed they were just friends, but she'd never known if things were truly innocent. And then there were all the times when he'd forgotten to call when he promised he would or to show up for a date. He'd even forgotten her birthday.

"And yet you hung in with him."

"Okay, I see your point," she grumbled. But it was different. Somehow. She recognized it in her gut. "I don't have a reason I can point to."

The way his lips thinned as he pressed them together infuriated her. What did he expect? She couldn't explain to him something she didn't understand herself.

"We could get to the bottom of it if we went to see someone."

Again, his offer made her blood freeze. She couldn't understand why. "Can it wait until after I've finished my album?"

"Of course." He sounded agreeable, but worry shadowed his expression. "But I think we need to do something in the meantime. That's why after we left the doctor's appointment earlier, I called a counselor in LA I trust."

Feeling ambushed, Melody demanded, "You talked to someone about our problems?"

"Relax," Kyle said. "She's someone I've been going to for years."

This bit of information came at Melody like a wrecking ball. "You see a therapist? How did I not know that?"

A muscle jumped in Kyle's cheek. "It's not something I'm proud of."

She knew what he meant. Because it made him look weak to need help. She opened her mouth to tell him that she didn't expect him to be strong all the time, but was that true? When he'd given her a glimpse of his insecurity where Hunter was concerned, she hadn't exactly been understanding of how he'd felt.

She liked being able to lean on Kyle. Appreciated how he took charge, made her feel safe and cared for. Since he rarely discussed his own troubles or difficulties, it never occurred to her that he might need to count on her support in return.

"Why didn't you tell me?" It worried her that she'd

failed him. "Is it because of your dad?" His father had taught him to appear strong.

"It's the sort of thing that would make him crazy." After a heartbeat his lips curved into a dry smile. "I'm not sure what would be worse for him. Having a problem or admitting there was something wrong. I'm sure he'd rather have his leg cut off than agree to see a therapist."

"That's pretty dramatic." Yet it wasn't much of an exaggeration.

"It's pretty indicative of how determined my father is to not show any weakness." Kyle's voice lightened despite his pained grimace. "So now you know one of my deep dark secrets."

"One of?" She smiled through her heavy heart. "How many more are there?"

"You'll have to take the next fourteen days and find out."

He'd just done exactly as she'd often longed for him to do and opened up. And not just with a little something. He'd admitted something deeply personal and all in the spirit of improving their communication. At the same time, he'd issued a challenge: *I'm all in, are you?*

"What do you mean the next fourteen days?"

"Dr. Warner gave me a step-by-step fourteen-day relationship revitalizer. I thought we could start with this right now."

Melody blew out a breath. Why was she so resistant to what Kyle was trying to do? Didn't she want them to get back together? Kyle was obviously making an effort. Shouldn't she as well?

"Okay," she said before she changed her mind. "Let's do this."

"I'm glad you're on board." And there was a little softening in his manner that suggested relief.

"Where do we begin?"

"Here is the list of what we do each of the fourteen days. I think it spells everything out pretty well." He handed her a seven-page document. "It looks like a lot, but when I explained about your album deadline, Dr. Warner said we don't have to commit to doing something fourteen days in a row."

Before starting to read, she flipped through all the pages. For some strange reason her chest tightened. This was a huge undertaking. Much more than she was ready to handle. When she thought of going to a couples counselor, she imagined just sitting in a room and talking around their problems. Not this.

"Day one," she read. "Praise and appreciation. Write thirty of your favorite things about your partner and share them."

This she could do. There were hundreds of things she appreciated about Kyle. Maybe this whole task wouldn't be as bad as she thought.

"How about we take the rest of today and tomorrow to make our lists and then have dinner tomorrow night and talk them over?" Kyle suggested.

It was on the tip of Melody's tongue to say she could fire them off in an hour, but then she considered that maybe he needed more time to find thirty things about her he liked. Her insides clenched at the thought that he might struggle with what to put on his list.

"That sounds great," she said.

After Kyle packed up the remains of their dinner and left the studio, Melody picked up her notebook, turned to a fresh sheet of paper and started to write thirty favorite things about Kyle. The first ten were easy. His eyes, smile, gorgeous body, his long fingers, deep voice, toe-curling kisses, his listening skills, the fact that he wanted to work on the relationship, his strong work ethic and support of her music career.

She sat back with a happy sigh and reviewed the list. Now, for the next ten. She wrote down several more of his exceptional body parts, his inability to carry a tune and his laugh. Her list had expanded to seventeen. Only thirteen more to go.

Melody stuck the pen in her mouth and worried the plastic until it was covered with teeth marks. Her mind was suddenly blank. Surely there were dozens and dozens more things about Kyle that she appreciated. Why couldn't she think of any?

Instead, she was bombarded by all the things that were wrong with him. The way he could talk endlessly about baseball stats, how he often worked with a game playing in the background. How he sometimes came home from business meetings and didn't want to talk. He insisted on maintaining a close connection with his family despite how much they frustrated him.

The door to the studio opened and Mia slipped inside. Her cheeks glowed rosy and her brown eyes sparkled. She'd obviously just come from seeing Nate. The two were so in love and for a second Melody struggled with envy.

"What are you working on?" Mia asked, coming to sit on the couch beside Melody.

"I'm supposed to be writing thirty of my favorite things about Kyle." She went on to explain about the relationship revitalization journey they were on.

"That sounds amazing. Nate and I should do that."

Melody gave her a wry look. "But you two are deliriously happy together. You don't need to revitalize anything."

"I think every couple could stand to deepen their connection no matter what stage the relationship is in."

While she mulled this over, Melody handed Mia the instructions Kyle had given her. Maybe if she and Kyle had done something like this in the beginning, instead of just counting on their sexual chemistry to drive the relationship, they wouldn't have drifted apart during those long months she spent on the road.

"'Day six,'" Mia read, her voice filled with delight. "'Sex—a spoiling session for her.' Now that sounds fantastic."

Melody's stomach dropped to her toes. Three hours earlier she'd been ready to have sex with Kyle again and yet now, instead of the idea sending thrills through her, she was awash in apprehension. Because day six wasn't about the physical act of sex, but about intimacy. And she sure wasn't ready for that.

Mia continued, "'Your partner gets to have a totally selfish block of time.'" Her eyes widened as she kept going. "'Thirty minutes to three hours. She gets to be totally in control of the environment and actions.' Oh, you lucky girl."

"Let me see that." Melody wanted to snatch the pages from Mia's hands and read it all herself. Instead, she stewed impatiently while Mia finished reading the instructions.

"And at the end are suggestions for what can happen during the spoiling session. If you don't mind I'd like to make a copy of this."

"Sure." Melody fell into a thoughtful mood as Mia left the control booth.

She turned her attention back to the list she was supposed to make. After adding some of his cute quirks and business acumen, she'd reached twenty. Well, at least she had another twenty-four hours before they were supposed to get together. Surely she could come up with ten more things she liked and appreciated about Kyle. And if she couldn't, maybe she was kidding herself that they could make this work.

Five

Instead of picking up Melody at the studio, he agreed to meet her at Batouri's restaurant in Fontaine Ciel on the Strip. He was already waiting at the bar when she walked in. The chandeliers dangling from the ceiling cast faceted light over her dark hair as she slipped onto the barstool beside him.

"Nice place," she commented, her gaze touring the gold pillars and black tables set with white china and crystal.

"Wait until you taste the food. Chef Croft is a culinary genius."

"I'm glad I brought my appetite."

Kyle frowned. "Did you eat today?"

He wasn't happy about her weight loss. She claimed

it was because of her morning sickness, but he wouldn't be surprised if stress had added to the problem.

"Breakfast, lunch and several snacks."

"Healthy ones?"

She gave him a stern look. "I'm not sure if you fussing over me is delightful or annoying."

"It's delightful," Kyle said. "Just like me."

"You're delightful?" Her lips twitched.

"When I put my mind to it." And he'd decided that was what he intended to do. "Come on, let's go see about our table."

Taking her hand, he led her to the hostess. He liked the way Melody's fingers curved around his. The contact reminded him of a time before the gap between them had grown so broad. Settling into a cozy booth, they placed their drink order, listened to that night's specials and waded into the shallow end with some small talk about her album.

"It's crazy, but now that I'm nearing the end, I'm in a love/hate relationship with every song. I can't be objective about any of them. Mia thinks I'm struggling to finish because I'm in love with making the album and I don't want the process to end. I keep telling her that I'm eager for it to be over."

"All of that makes sense. It's a huge undertaking. Have you given much thought to what you're going to do to celebrate?"

"Not a clue. I've been so caught up in putting all the finishing touches on everything that I haven't pictured what the coming weeks will hold."

"Some much-needed rest and relaxation," Kyle suggested, hoping she'd consider returning to LA with him.

Savannah's movie was wrapping in the next few weeks and she and Trent would be returning to Las Vegas. That meant Kyle's stint at Club T's was over. He had his business interests in LA to return to.

But he wasn't going anywhere without Melody.

"How did you find our first exercise?" Melody asked as the waitress delivered her salad and Kyle's steak.

"Are you asking me if I had a hard time thinking up thirty things about you I like?"

In fact, the exercise had been remarkably easy.

"Yes."

"Not at all. There are hundreds of things about you that I appreciate."

She scowled at him, but he could tell she liked what he had to say. "Are any of them not sexual?"

"Quite a few. Would you like me to pull out my list and get started?"

"Sure." She got her own list out of her purse and flattened the folded sheet on the black tabletop beside her plate. "Do you want to start or should I?"

"Ladies first." He thought a second before adding, "Why don't we alternate."

"Let's see." Her eyes scanned down her list as if searching for the perfect place to begin.

He shook his head. "From the top. I want to know what your first thoughts of me were."

Her cheeks grew pink and she squirmed in her seat. "Your eyes. I never know what color they will be from one moment to the next. It's something about the light or what you're wearing. And there's nothing I enjoy more than looking up and catching you watching me from across a room."

Kyle decided this was an excellent beginning. "Your determination," he said, taking his turn. "Since you were a teenager, you've written music, despite your father's attempts to dissuade you. Even though it hasn't been easy to overcome Siggy's negative attitudes, you chose your path and you've been successful."

His words made her smile. Good. That was what he was going for.

"Your smile," she said after a quick glance at her sheet. "Sometimes you come home and I can tell your day has been trying. But then you look at me and smile and it's as if the sun comes out."

Kyle made a note to smile around her more often. "Your talent. Both your songwriting and your singing. I am constantly impressed by your lyrics and music. Makes me wish I could carry a tune."

"That's farther down on my list," she said excitedly. "Your inability to carry a tune."

He made a face at her. "Why would someone with perfect pitch find that attractive?"

"Because it means you're not perfect." There was such an eager note in her voice.

"I'm the farthest thing from perfect and you know it."

"Well, but…"

She rolled her lips between her teeth, a sure sign she was thinking hard. Was she struggling for a way to spin his flaws in a positive light? Kyle waited her out. When Dr. Warner had spoken to him about the exercises in this relationship revitalizer, she'd made sure to point out that he needed to listen to what Melody had to say. It was something he hadn't done after finding out she'd been in New York with Hunter.

"You are handsome, rock a sexy body, have a full head of soft wavy hair, kissable lips, great legs. Don't get me started on your abs." Her words tumbled over one another as she rushed on.

As she listed off his physical attributes, he couldn't help but chuckle. It was nice to know the sexual chemistry was alive and well. He didn't plan to rely on sex to save their relationship, but maybe their desire for each other would compel them to work through all the tough stuff.

"Your voice on the phone gets me hot and in person…" She shook her head ruefully. "It's nice that you can't sing. It makes me feel like I can keep up with you."

"How many things on your list did you just read off?" he asked.

She scanned her list. "I might've gotten a little carried away. But there are lots of other things about you that I appreciate. Your sense of humor. Your business acumen. That you are such a good friend to my brother. I know things would've been a lot harder with my dad if Trent hadn't had you to talk to."

When she paused for breath Kyle jumped in.

"I admire how you've coped with a father as difficult as Siggy. And I remember what a hard time you had when your mother left you with him after the divorce."

Melody grimaced. "We've both been through a lot with our families."

"It's made us pretty gun-shy." Was it any wonder that neither one of them reacted well to their first major dustup.

"Can I tell you something without you getting upset?" she asked him.

"Of course." No matter what she had to say he would not take offense.

"When I was making this list, I got sidetracked into some things that I didn't like about you."

Kyle was amused by how horrified she was to admit this. "You don't think I know there are things about me that drive you crazy." He paused, thinking about his jealous reaction to her continued connection with Hunter. "Like everything baseball."

"You are obsessed." She exhaled as if his reaction, or lack of one, was a huge relief. "I just found it interesting that even though I didn't mean to I couldn't think about the good without thinking about the bad."

"Nobody is one thing or another. Although I think it's human nature to dwell on what's wrong rather than focus on what's good or right." It was something he'd done a lot of while they'd been apart.

"I'm glad we did this exercise. It really opened my eyes to who you are and why I fell in love with you."

"And also why you stayed away?" he prompted.

"A bit. I've been pretty overwhelmed these last few months. The tour took more out of me physically and emotionally than I realized and then I was nonstop writing, recording and producing my album." Her smile came and went. "Not to mention the fact that I'm pregnant and that has made me a little more reactionary than usual."

Kyle reached across the table and took her hand. "So shall we consider this exercise successfully accomplished?"

"I think we should." Her beautiful smile bloomed. "I'm happy with the results."

So was he. Kyle only hoped the next thirteen exercises went as well.

A huge yawn seized Melody just as she was pulling into the third stall in Trent's garage and she almost bumped up against the back wall. She shouldn't have stayed at the studio so late. In the last hour and a half she hadn't accomplished much of anything. Her mind kept wandering back to the prior evening with Kyle.

After the dinner had gone so well, neither one had been in a hurry for the night to end. They'd strolled through the extensive grounds behind the three interconnected Fontaine Resort hotels for almost two hours, talking about everything and nothing. She'd told him about her favorite parts of the tour and how much fun she'd had watching Nate and Mia fall in love. They rehashed what each knew about Trent's clever takeover of his family's company, West Coast Records. After seeing her back to her car, Kyle had given her a friendly kiss on the forehead and she'd driven away feeling achy and unsatisfied.

Now weariness dragged at her as she slipped through the door that led into the side yard, following the softly lit path to the guest cottage. Trent had spent a fortune landscaping the nearly one-acre backyard, tucking lights in every nook and cranny. Pathways, shrubs and trees were softly illuminated. The Monday after Thanksgiving, he'd hired a crew to wrap colored Christmas lights around the palm trees and fill the empty spaces on the lawn with lighted reindeer pulling Santa's sled and a train. For the past two days workers had been bustling around like elves.

He was pulling out all the stops both here and in LA so his son would have a memorable Christmas. Melody had refrained from pointing out that Dylan was only a year old and wouldn't remember any of it. Why spoil anything for Trent. He deserved to be happy. So did Savannah. Melody wanted nothing but the best for both of them. They'd traveled a long path to arrive at their destination.

Melody wondered if she and Kyle would ever get back to a place where they looked at each other with the sort of dreamy lust that marked the nonverbal exchanges between Trent and Savannah. For her part, she couldn't stop guarding her emotions. She wanted to trust Kyle, but was afraid if she opened herself up, he would say something that disappointed her. It was no way to build a relationship. But she couldn't figure out how to move on.

A large basket, wrapped in cellophane, sat on the porch beside the front door. She stared at it in wonder. How had he gotten here? Kyle had keys to Trent's house as well as the gate code to let himself into the backyard. Had he put it here as a surprise for her? As she drew closer, she could see baby items through the clear plastic wrap. Her heart gave a funny little leap.

She unlocked her front door and brought the basket inside, setting it on the dining room table where the roses had sat until Thanksgiving night when she and Kyle had argued over them.

A ribbon held the plastic wrap closed. The knot wouldn't yield to her fingers, so she fetched a pair of small scissors. Until she told Kyle about the baby, Melody hadn't been able to start planning for her future. Once they'd gone to the ultrasound and she'd seen the child growing inside of her, her nerves had transformed into flutters of excitement. But still, she hadn't started buying any of the multitude of things a baby would need. It was too early. Besides, shopping would be more fun if she shared the experience with Kyle.

The wrapping fell away and Melody admired the collection of onesies, bibs, tiny socks and books. And there was an adorable teddy bear. All the clothes were in neutral shades of yellow and green as if the giver didn't know the sex of the child. Did that mean Kyle hadn't given her the basket? Surely he would've chosen something in shades of pink to celebrate their baby girl.

She quickly checked over everything, but still didn't find a card. Another anonymous gift like the flowers. What the heck was going on? Should she be worried? Especially the way the basket had appeared on her doorstep. On the other hand, there could be a simple explanation. Savannah and Trent knew she'd told Kyle. Maybe they'd had the basket delivered. A quick way to find out would be to give them a call. Melody dialed Savannah's number. She didn't want to upset her brother for no reason.

"How is the filming going?" She asked when her sister-in-law answered.

"Pretty good. Just a few more scenes before we wrap. It's been a lot of fun. I really miss acting."

Savannah had been working in New York City first as a model and then an actress on a soap opera for several years before giving it up and returning to LA. She'd put her career on pause when she'd become pregnant and married Melody's brother Rafe. Now, two years, one baby boy and a deceased husband later, Savannah had accepted a supporting role in a movie and married Melody's other brother, Trent.

"I imagine I'd have a hard time giving up singing now that I've gotten a taste for it." Was that a choice she was going to have to make? She could name several women with huge music careers and families.

"Maybe you won't have to. I'm sure you and Kyle can work something out."

Would Kyle expect her to stay close to home? Before going out with Nate and Free Fall she'd never imagined herself a big star. And it would take a lot of hard work and personal sacrifice to get there. Was she ready for that?

"It's going to be a lot more complicated now that I'm having a baby. I guess if I tour, I'm gonna have to go for shorter periods of time."

The thought of being on the road and tearing apart her daughter and Kyle even for a few months made her queasy. And what if he sued her for partial custody and it was her separated from her baby. Her thoughts returned to his proposal. It had been more practical than romantic and so unlike him. While they'd been dating and even after she'd moved in, he showered dozens of sweet gestures on her.

It was why she'd thought he'd sent the roses. She'd been shaking with excitement as she opened the card. That it hadn't been signed by him had snatched away her delight for the briefest of seconds. He'd given her roses before, although his romantic style was more low-key and subtle. A handwritten note stuffed among her lingerie. A case of her favorite bottled water delivered to her while on tour.

Kyle made his feelings for her known in practical ways. The biggest one being how he supported her career and acted as a buffer between her and her father. She didn't need big drama to prove how much he cared for her.

But wouldn't it be nice if the baby basket was from him?

"Something showed up on my doorstep today," Melody said, "and I was wondering if you or Trent had anything to do with it."

"I didn't, but Trent might have. What was it?"

"A basket of baby things. There was no card. I thought maybe…" Melody felt foolish.

"Kyle must've sent it. No one else beside us knows that you're pregnant, right?"

"I said something to a couple people at the studio." Melody relaxed. Maybe Mia had organized something and sent the gift. But why no card?

"That is very nice of them. Now I feel bad that Trent and I haven't done anything for you."

"Don't be ridiculous," Melody said, gazing around the beautiful guesthouse. "You've been supportive and Trent is letting me stay here rent-free."

"You know you're welcome to stay as long as you need." Savannah's voice took on a note of concern. "Now that Kyle knows about the baby, have you thought about moving back in with him? Not that we want you to go, we just want you two back the way you were."

"We talked about it a little." Melody huffed out a laugh. "In fact he proposed. Before you get all excited, I turned him down."

"Why? You love him and you're having his baby."

But did he love her in return?

"It was more in the vein of *hey, you're pregnant, we should make it legal*. He hadn't thought it through. And before he found out about the baby he was pretty clear he thought we should break up."

"That's not the impression I got."

"He jumped to the conclusion I was cheating on him based on a paparazzi photo," Melody reminded her. "He's known me over ten years. He should've realized I would never start one relationship without ending another."

"You sort of started something with him while you were dating Hunter."

"We were pretending. Our feelings might've gotten out of hand, but Kyle and I never kissed or did anything that crossed the line."

"I think he loves you and doesn't know how to handle such strong feelings. His dad is such a control freak. Kyle never really had a chance to be open and intimate with anyone before you came along."

"I know. He was an emotional fortress. Still is sometimes." Most of the time, Melody thought, wishing she'd stayed in LA and nurtured their fledgling relationship instead of taking off for nine months. "Some of it is his dad. Some of it is the women he met when he was a ballplayer. They wanted the lifestyle his money could provide. When we first started dating and I was trying to get him to open up, he often mentioned that they were disingenuous. He didn't know who he could trust."

"Well, he knows he can trust you," Savannah said. "Oh, dear, looks like my boys need me. Give Kyle our love and you stay strong. And if you ever figure out who gave you the basket, let me know."

Melody hung up with Savannah and stared at the phone for a few minutes before dialing Kyle's number. Maybe it was time she stopped making excuses for keeping him at arm's length and start figuring out if they had a future.

Six

Several days passed after their dinner to exchange their favorite things about each other, before Kyle and Melody were able to get together for the second exercise: romantic massage. The thought of getting to put his hands on Melody and vice versa had preoccupied him for the last couple of days. Seeing the way she'd been logging hours at the studio he'd expected to wait. Therefore, he was delighted when she phoned him from the studio one day—Nate had found her sleeping in one of the control booths and told her to go home. She'd called Kyle to ask if they could meet and he'd quickly agreed.

She'd chosen to come to his house in the early afternoon before he had to be at Club T's. When his doorbell sounded, Kyle hadn't yet settled on what part of his body he wanted her hands on. They'd agreed that each got to choose one part to massage on the other person and also which part they wanted massaged on their own body. He'd decided to lavish his attention on her hands.

"What all do you have there?" he asked.

"It's a foot spa." She carried a large plastic tub and had a heavy tote bag slung over her shoulder. "I'm giving you a pedicure and foot massage." She said it like she expected him to argue.

"Okay." The notion of her kneeling at his feet was a definite turn-on. Unfortunately that wasn't what this particular exercise was about. "And what part of you am I massaging?"

"I haven't decided yet."

"Maybe we should put body parts in a hat and draw."

She smiled at his suggestion. "That's not a bad idea." She carried her supplies into his living room and placed everything in front of a chair. "Do you mind putting some water on to boil?"

"Are you planning on cooking my feet?"

"No, but I want the water to be extra warm so you relax." She cocked her head and looked at him. "Have you ever had a pedicure?"

He shook his head. "One of the guys on the team used to get them all the time and got the nickname Twinkle Toes because of it."

"That's terrible," Melody said, but her scolding would have been more effective without the amused smile. "You shouldn't ignore your feet. They deserve to be pampered just as much as every other part of your body. More so, because they take the most punishment, lugging around our weight all day."

"I see your point."

From his vantage in the kitchen, he watched her pull a perplexing collection of items out of her bag, from clippers to lotions to some sort of scrubber. He was half expecting her to produce a bottle of red nail polish. No, she wouldn't do that to him.

"How's the water coming?"

"Almost ready to boil. Do you need me to fill the tub with warmish water?"

She was arranging a towel on the tile to soak up any spillage and glanced up with a smile that caused a spike in his heart rate. "That would be great."

Ten minutes later, she had things arranged to her satisfaction and made him go put on shorts. Soft instrumental music poured from the speakers set into the ceiling, adding to the spa-like feel she had created. He sat down and slipped his feet into the spa tub. As the hot, bubbly water enveloped his feet and the vibrating massagers worked their way along his arches, he got a sense of what old Twinkle Toes had been about.

"Relaxed?" she asked, adding something fragrant to the water that had an immediate impact on his blood pressure.

"That smells great." A low noise left his throat as tension he didn't even realize he'd been carrying fell away. "What is it?"

"Lavender." She tapped his right shin. "Let's start with this one."

He lifted the foot free of water and she dried it off before setting it on the towel in her lap. While she got to work with clippers and some sort of manicure scissors that tickled his skin, he stared at her bent head and let himself appreciate her.

Once she had his toenails trimmed to her satisfaction, she began to work lotion into his feet and calf muscles. From playing the violin and piano, she had strong fingers. And she knew exactly where to apply pressure to best effect.

"That's amazing," he groaned, closing his eyes and letting his head drop back. "Where did you learn to do that?"

"On tour," she said. "I'd come offstage after a set and my feet would be killing me. One of the guys in Free Fall gave the most incredible foot massages."

"Should I be jealous?" In truth, at the moment he couldn't conjure the tiniest flicker of concern.

"He was happily married with three kids. Apparently his wife runs marathons and he's learned how to take care of her feet."

"Lucky woman." However, her comment made him aware that he and Melody hadn't been the only two people separated by the tour. Maybe they'd just been the least prepared to deal with the lengthy time apart.

He considered asking her how the other band members and their significant others coped with the separation, but that was a question for another time. Right now, he just wanted to sit back and enjoy the feel of her soft, strong hands turning his bones to oatmeal.

"How do you feel?" She asked him twenty minutes

later. Her eyes glowed as she observed the effect of her ministrations on him.

"Call me Twinkle Toes," he said. "I'm sold."

She laughed and there was such delight in it. More than the relaxing massage, this was his reward.

"Next time," she promised. "I'll give you a facial."

If he wasn't careful, she'd turn him into a hedonist. On the other hand maybe that wasn't such a bad thing. Maybe he should arrange for a couples massage as a special treat when she put her album to bed and could relax enough to enjoy it.

"Thank you." He pulled her into his arms for a quick hug that quickly escalated into something more as she wrapped her arms around him and held on.

In the early days of their relationship, he'd been so caught up in his body's need for her that he hadn't taken the time he should've to get to know her romantic side. Instead, it had been easier to learn what made her body writhe and where to touch her to tear moans from her throat.

At the start lust had a fierce hold on him. But as the months wore on and his craving for her didn't so much diminish as change, he'd realized for the first time in his life he was caught up in something dangerous and delightful.

"This feels amazing," he began, wondering how to extricate himself without upsetting her. "But after three months without you, I'm more than a little hard up. And we have to get to day six before there's any sex allowed." He cupped her butt and held her firmly against him, letting her feel his arousal. It wasn't a request for sex, but a way to seek her sympathy.

"Are you sure you want to wait?"

At his fierce growl, she laughed and arched her back, rocking her hips and lightly grinding herself against him. The sharp bite of desire caused pain to flare, but not where Kyle would've expected. When her softly rounded stomach grazed against his lower abdomen, his heart gave a mighty wrench. This so shocked him that he stepped back instead of going in for a mind-blowing kiss.

Cursing, he rubbed his hands over his face.

"Kyle?" Melody caught at his hands and pulled them down so she could see his expression. Her eyes darkened as she regarded him. "Are you okay?"

"Yeah," he said, cursing the uncertainty in her gaze. The last thing he wanted was for her to feel less than safe with him. Summoning a lopsided grin, he rubbed his chin. "It's just that I go from zero to a million around you." He glanced down at the front of his shorts. "You deserve better."

"There's nothing wrong with a little down-and-dirty sex." Her lashes fluttered down to hide the glint in her eyes. "Once upon a time we fell on each other like hormonally charged teenagers."

"That was before you got pregnant." And before he'd overreacted to her being with Hunter in New York instead of talking through the situation.

"What does my being pregnant have to do with anything?"

He made a vague gesture in the direction of her stomach. "It's more than just the two of us now."

"Kyle, are you telling me you're going to be shy in front of our unborn baby?"

This conversation was not going the way he wanted it to. "It's not about being shy. It's about being careful."

"Careful?" Now she wasn't even trying to conceal her amusement. "How exactly do you plan on being careful?"

Damn her. He didn't have an answer. Mostly because he hadn't thought the whole thing through. When he remained silent, grappling for how to respond, she made a rude noise.

"Pregnant women have been having sex since the dawn of time. I read that during the second trimester as the nausea fades, hormones increase our sex drive."

"Please stop."

"In fact," she said as if he hadn't spoken, "many women engage in sex to stimulate labor."

Kyle was desperate to put an end to the topic of sex. His shorts were uncomfortably tight and thinking about naked Melody, sprawled on his sheets, her belly round with his child, wasn't helping matters one bit.

"Your turn. Have you figured out what you'd like me to do for you? We could refill the basin and I could return the favor."

She shook her head. "I had a pedicure the other day." Her lashes came down to shadow her eyes. "I suppose you could do my shoulders. They're pretty tight at the moment."

"How about I start with your hands and work my way up to your shoulders?"

Her eyes brightened. "Sure. That sounds nice and I have some really great cream I just bought."

He drew her to a chaise longue and sat down with her between his thighs, her back to him. While she relaxed back against his chest, he took the cream and utilized some of the techniques she'd demonstrated on his feet, sliding his thumbs deep into the flesh of her palms.

"That feels really good," she said, her head falling back against his shoulder.

She'd stripped down to a tank. Her breath slipped out in a happy sigh as his fingers traced up her arms and over her shoulders. He loved the way she fit against him. All soft, yielding curves and warm, enticing energy.

He thought they were getting somewhere until her phone rang. The discordant sound caused her to tense.

"Ignore it," he murmured, kissing the side of her neck. "This is our time."

"I really can't." She shifted forward and quickly moved beyond his grasp. "There's this one song I really love, but I can't quite get it right." She checked her phone's display and turned her back to him. "Hey, thanks for calling me back. Do you have some time later?"

Now Kyle was the one growing tense. From her body language and tone he knew exactly who was calling. Hunter. She shot a look over her shoulder in Kyle's direction.

"Ah, sure, I can meet you in an hour. Thanks, I really appreciate it."

"I thought Nate told you to take the rest of the day off."

"He did, but there's a really small window of opportunity…" She slipped her shirt over her head and once again donned her sweater. Moving with more speed than grace she began to gather up all that she'd brought.

Kyle stood with his arms crossed and watched her. "That was Hunter, wasn't it?"

"Please don't make a big deal out of this," she pleaded. "It's really just about my album."

He couldn't help but think she wouldn't be running off if it wasn't for Hunter. "Why aren't you going to Nate for help?"

She wouldn't meet his gaze. "I have gone to him. And to Mia. I just want another opinion."

It was obvious that she was drowning in self-doubt. This album was her chance to prove to herself and the world she was a talented singer and songwriter. But more than that, deep down, part of her would forever be that starry-eyed teenager whose dreams had been trampled by her father's brutal words.

"I understand." She would never know what it cost him to say that. "But before you leave, can we please agree we'll do date night on Wednesday?"

"Wednesday is perfect. Nate has given me a deadline of noon. After that…" She smiled through her anxiety. "I'm all yours."

* * *

When the door to the rehearsal studio opened, Melody looked up and spied Nate. He frowned at her.

"Weren't you supposed to be out of here two hours ago?"

"I've been working on this song for Ivy Bliss."

She'd gotten caught up in working on something she shouldn't be. Hunter had called around noon and asked for some changes to a song Ivy Bliss had started to record before switching to work with Hunter a month ago. Apparently, thanks to Hunter, she was back to being interested in the song again. But she wanted two new verses. Melody had been fiddling with the song all afternoon instead of working on her own album. Hunter was in LA tomorrow to work with Ivy and wanted the song today so they could look it over.

"Wait," Melody said, as something Nate had asked just penetrated her creative fog. "Did you say two hours ago? What time is it?"

"Nearly four. I thought you and Kyle had some big dinner planned for tonight."

"I lost track of time." This was not good.

Today was day three of their relationship revitalization and they were supposed to have date night. The plan had been for her to head to his house at two. They were going grocery shopping and then would return to his place to prepare a four-course dinner. The point of the exercise was spending time together engaged in something fun and cooperative.

"What song?" Nate asked, bringing her thoughts back to the moment.

"The one you and Mia suggested she do. She wants me to change a couple verses."

Nate shook his head. He knew the demanding pop star all too well. Not only had she been on tour with his band Free Fall, he was currently engaged to her sister.

"Want me to take a look?" he asked.

Relief washed through Melody with such intensity that tears sprung to her eyes. "That would be great. Hunter wants to look at the new verses today. I don't know that they're any good. I'm absolutely drained of all creative energy."

To her relief, Nate didn't scold her, although he sure looked like he wanted to. Mia was also pregnant, so Nate understood how exhausted an expectant mother could get.

"Give me your notes and Mia and I will put our heads together. Go have dinner with Kyle."

"Thank you."

She'd left her phone in her purse while she worked. It was in the corner of the room under her jacket. As soon as Nate left the room, she went to dig it out.

At two, when she realized the project for Hunter wasn't going well, she'd called Kyle and explained that she needed some extra time in the studio. She hadn't revealed that she was working on something for Hunter. Kyle would not appreciate having his date night usurped by her ex-boyfriend.

Sure enough, there were two calls and several texts over the last half hour. She'd promised him she'd be there at three. Now it was four. No doubt he was frantic. Ironically, showing up late or not at all was the exact sort of thing that had driven her crazy about Hunter. She'd hated how his tardiness had made her feel so low on his priority scale. Now she was doing the same thing to Kyle.

"Sorry, I lost track of time," she said when he answered the phone. "I'm leaving the studio now."

"I'm just glad to hear your voice and know that you're okay." He sounded less tense as he went along. "I don't know how hungry you are, but we might have to bag what we planned to go for something simpler."

She'd been in charge of finding a dish that was straightforward enough for them to handle, but time-consuming in its preparation. She'd settled on a recipe for baked tortellini pie that sounded fantastic. She and Kyle shared a love of all sorts of Italian foods.

Leaving Ivy's song in Nate's and Mia's capable hands, she headed to Kyle's place. Traffic was worse than usual and it took her half an hour to get there. Now, at four thirty, there wasn't time to make all the tortellini from scratch, create the ragu, roll out the pastry dough as well as make the almond soup and the flourless chocolate torte for dessert.

"I was thinking about the shrimp scampi over angel hair pasta we made the first night I stayed over at your place," she said, hoping the fond memory would alleviate some of the disappointment she saw shadowed in Kyle's hazel eyes.

"With some crusty bread and something decadent for dessert."

She had to give him credit for trying to seem upbeat. "Sounds perfect."

They got in his car and headed for the grocery store near his house. It was a boutique market with specialty cheeses and meats, fresh-baked bread and all sorts of fun and interesting edibles. After loading up with angel hair pasta, shrimp, lemons and garlic, they headed to the bakery for bread and decided to buy a tiramisu and a death-by-chocolate cake instead of trying to make something.

She was sampling an olive tapenade when her phone started ringing. Kyle was several feet away, looking at the infused olive oils. She decided to risk checking who was calling. To her relief, it was Mia. She answered.

"I love the changes you've made," Mia said. "Ivy will, too, I imagine. Nate and I tweaked a couple things here and there. Do you want me to send you the updated version?"

As curious as she was, Melody was leery of letting work interrupt any more of her date night with Kyle. "No, I trust you. Do you mind sending it to Hunter?"

"No problem. You kids have fun."

"Who is that?"

Melody whipped around and realized Kyle was standing right beside her. "Mia, telling me to have fun tonight." Her stomach clenched at the half lie, but what Kyle didn't know wouldn't ruin their evening. "Are you ready to check out?"

Fifteen minutes later, they were back at Kyle's house. Melody put classical music on the stereo—Kyle had balked at Italian opera—and together they made quick work of the shrimp cleaning. Standing side by side, they chopped greens, zested a lemon and started boiling the pasta. While their ingredients sizzled in a skillet on the stove, Kyle set the table and poured the basil-infused olive oil into small dishes for them to dip their warmed bread into. In no time at all, plates loaded with pasta and shrimp were heading for the table.

Since he was renting the house, she hadn't expected such a well turned-out table, including china place settings, crystal goblets filled with juice instead of wine and silver candleholders. He'd even bought a bouquet of bright flowers for a centerpiece.

"This is lovely," she exclaimed, feeling slightly guilty that he'd prepared for their date while she'd made it a lower priority.

"You taught me a lot about setting the mood."

In the months they'd lived together, she made sure they had a couple romantic dinners a week. Their schedules were often hectic and she'd wanted to make certain they took time to focus on each other and made dinner a special event.

Sometimes it had bothered her that Kyle didn't seem to appreciate the extra bit of work that went into their dinners. Now, she was seeing that he'd noticed and understood what she'd been trying to do even if he'd never commented on it.

"Is it as good as you remember?" Melody asked around a mouthful of succulent garlicky goodness.

He moaned in response and the sound was so inviting that a fire kindled in Melody's lower half. She should've added the sounds he made during sex to her list of things she appreciated about him. With a sigh, she focused her carnal appetites on the food in front of her. Day six couldn't come soon enough.

"Ready for dessert?" she asked after they'd cleared the table and done the dishes.

She was in a mellow mood from the delicious food and thoroughly entertained by Kyle's Club T's stories about some of the crazy things customers had done. Everything from deliberate wardrobe malfunctions to brawling to couples engaging in sex challenges. As if by mutual agreement, they avoided bringing up anything that would result in an argument. Such as Hunter or their future plans.

"Hmm. Dessert," Kyle murmured, cupping her face in his long fingers and tilting her head to the perfect angle.

As he slanted his lips over hers, sensation shimmered and then spread through her entire body until she felt bathed in joy. He'd always had that effect on her, even before she'd understood that in her subconscious mind he'd crossed from being an old family friend to a man she very much desired.

His tongue slid over hers, relearning her mouth. It was a soft, questing kiss. One meant to draw her out instead of claim her. It made it easy to relax and breathe him in. To absorb the warmth of his hands and let the memories unfold in her mind of all the kisses they'd shared. He asked her for nothing more than to revel in this moment with him.

She almost moaned in dismay when his lips lifted from hers. But he wasn't done with her. His uneven breath tickled her skin as he seized her earlobe between his teeth, awakening a shudder.

"That was nice." Melody breathed in his clean, masculine scent and held on like he was a life preserver and she was a woman in the middle of the ocean.

"So very nice. You taste way better than any dessert," Kyle said, claiming her mouth once again. This time his hands moved over her with deliberate intent, but just as she was ready to surrender to jumping ahead to day six, he lifted his lips from her. "Do you want coffee as well?"

"Coffee?" she moaned as his hands fell away. "Just what I need, to be jacked up on caffeine all night so I can stay awake and think about that kiss."

Kyle's smile grew wicked.

"I have decaf," he said

"Lovely." She exhaled her disappointment. "Brew away."

Her phone began to ring insistently from her purse as she cut slices of tiramisu and chocolate cake. By mutual agreement, they'd put away their phones for the duration of their evening. Unfortunately, Melody had neglected to turn hers off. She didn't realize she'd stopped working and was staring toward the source of the sound until Kyle spoke.

"Do you want to get that?"

"No." She finished putting their dessert on plates and carried them to the living room where Kyle had flipped on the fireplace. "I'm sure it's nothing."

And for about five minutes she forgot all about the call as the chocolate cake melted on her tongue. But when her phone began to ring a second time, she twitched in dismay at another interruption.

"Sorry, I should've turned it off the first time," Melody said, getting to her feet. The screen said it was Hunter calling. She winced and shut the phone down. "There, we shouldn't have any more interruptions."

"Who was it?" Kyle asked with studied indifference.

"No one important." She picked up her plate again. "You know that corner right there would be perfect for a Christmas tree. We should get you one."

Kyle's expression grew serious. "I was planning to be back in LA for Christmas."

"But…" What should she say to that? "I thought you'd want to spend Christmas with me."

"I do," he said, his gaze trailing away from her toward her purse. "In our house. In LA."

"Your house," she corrected automatically, startled by the sudden revelation. Not once had she considered his LA house her home. She'd never let herself settle in. It was almost as if she'd half expected their relationship would one day end. "And all my family will be here."

By that she meant Trent, Savannah, Dylan, Nate and Mia. Even though the last two weren't technically related to her, she'd come to think of them as more than just friends.

"I guess that answers my question as to where you're planning to stay once you have the baby."

"That's not fair." She hadn't made any sort of decision. In truth, she was still running scared. "I don't want to fight about this tonight."

"Who was on the phone, Melody?" he asked again, this time with a tone of calm authority.

With a burst of irritation, she decided to tell him. The evening was falling apart anyway. "Hunter." She debated whether or not she should explain the reason and Kyle's flat expression told her it might damage their efforts to reconnect if she let him think the worst. "Ivy Bliss wants to record one of my songs, but needed some new verses so I was working on them earlier today."

"And the reason Hunter called you?"

"I don't know. Just before I came over tonight, I gave Mia and Nate the song to work on and she sent the updated verses onto Hunter. Maybe he was calling to say he liked them or that he hated them. I don't know." Realizing she was breathing too hard, Melody knit her fingers together and struggled for calm. "Hunter and I have a professional relationship. You're just going to need to accept that."

"Or else?" he prompted in a silky tone.

There was no "or else." She wasn't trying to shove an ultimatum at him. "I'm really tired. Maybe I need to go."

She got to her feet, scooped up her purse and headed for the front door. Silence filled the space she'd just vacated. The temptation to turn around and say something clawed at her. But what more could she say? And then she was at his door. Cool air struck her hot cheeks as she stepped across the threshold.

"Don't go." Kyle's voice came from right behind her. "I'm sorry that I acted like such an idiot about you and Hunter working together."

She was so preoccupied by her thoughts that she hadn't noticed he'd followed her. Melody's heart knocked against her ribs and she tried unsuccessfully to swallow the lump in her throat.

She turned in Kyle's direction and saw the pain in his eyes. That he was being open about his hurt and regret was such a shock. She considered how seriously he was taking these exercises and thought of the romantic table setting. He'd been looking forward to their evening.

"I'm sorry I was late to our date," she said. "Working through our problems is important to me. I don't want you to think that it's not."

"You've got a lot on your plate right now. And that's really exciting news about Ivy Bliss wanting to record one of your songs." He offered her a gentle smile as he took her hand and tugged her toward him "Why don't you come back inside and tell me all about it while I clean up the kitchen."

"I can help with that," she offered, feeling as if she owed him for her tardiness.

"No, you will sit and watch me while I work." When she opened her mouth to protest he shook his head. "You're just going to have to get used to letting me take care of you."

Even as she nodded, she realized that he'd been taking care of her in one way or another for as long as she could remember. The question was what had she done for him in return?

Seven

After how things had gone on day three's date night, it was two days before Kyle reached out to Melody again. Deciding to find neutral territory for day four's communication exercise, he suggested Club T's on Monday afternoon. The forty-thousand-square-foot nightclub wasn't open for business until evening. One perk about being part owner and the current manager was that he had the keys to the place.

"I've never been in here when it's been empty," Melody said. "I kinda like it."

"It's not exactly intimate." Fourteen thousand square feet inside, another twenty-six thousand outside including the pool. "Although there are some nooks and crannies we could sneak off into."

"It's such a beautiful day," she said, flashing a

smile. The temperatures had climbed into the mid-sixties. "I was hoping we could sit out by the pool."

"Of course. Let me grab some drinks and we can head out there."

The first three dates had held mixed results. One thing was for sure: anything having to do with touching, they were going to excel at. It also shed light on the fact that they'd been using physical intimacy as a crutch. They'd moved too fast from dating to living together to being parents.

Circling the pool were side-by-side lounges with thick mattresses and backrests that could be lowered flat. Once Melody chose where she wanted to sit, Kyle spun one of the lounges so that they could face each other rather than recline side by side.

"Are you ready to dive into communication?" Melody asked. After that day-three-date-night debacle, she was demonstrating more willingness to participate in the exercises.

"First question," Kyle said. "How can I love you best?"

Since he'd never actually told her that he loved her, this question made both of them wince. She glanced down at her hands, noticed herself playing with her long sweater and clasped her fingers together in her lap.

"How about you answer first," she suggested.

Kyle suspected she was playing for time. "First off, you've committed to fourteen days of relationship revitalization and that's wonderful. I would like for you to talk to me when you're upset about something instead of shutting down all communication."

Melody's lips tightened minutely, but she nodded. "I want to feel secure with you."

The hardest thing about this exercise was to stay silent while she spoke. Kyle gave an encouraging nod even as his insides turned to stone. He knew what she wanted. For him to tell her he loved her. And he did love her, but telling her while they remained at odds wouldn't give her the satisfaction she believed it would. She wouldn't trust that he meant what he said; she'd just suspect he was mouthing the words to facilitate their reconciliation. The time to tell her he loved her had been before she left on the tour and every day after.

"That doesn't mean I expect you to ask me to marry you or even to tell me you love me. It means I want you to trust me about Hunter."

He should've seen it coming. His distrust was what had created their current situation. After seeing her hand-in-hand with her ex-boyfriend, Kyle had never stopped to question why he'd assumed she'd go back to Hunter.

"Where Hunter is concerned, I trust you completely." What he didn't trust was Hunter and his attempts to worm his way back into Melody's life. "Next question. How do I support you in a meaningful way? How can I support you better?"

"You've always been behind me with my music. Even when it tore us apart, you encouraged me to pursue it. You know how hard it was for me growing up with my dad being so negative about my abilities as a singer and a songwriter. I can never thank you enough for not just letting me go but for welcoming me back."

He nodded. Would he do the same thing again knowing how hard it would be to be apart from her for so many months? Probably. She was developing into such a talented performer that to clip her wings would be a crime. In the last year she'd blossomed, both as an artist and as a woman. No man who truly deserved her love would want anything less than the best for her.

"And how can I support you better?"

"Sometimes I think you're a little too understanding."

"What?" That was the last thing he expected to hear her say. Especially after the way he reacted every time Hunter's name was mentioned. "I don't know what you mean."

"How happy were you when I went off on tour?"

"For you, very. For me, not at all."

"I think your support of my music is a double-edged sword. On one hand, you're the understanding guy who encourages and believes in me when I don't. That's such an amazing gift. On the other hand, because of how my dad was about my music, you treat me like I'm fragile and don't give me good boundaries."

"What are you getting at?"

"The tour with Free Fall." She wrinkled her nose. "Looking back, I wish you'd asked me to only do part of it."

"You'd have been okay with that?" Kyle wished they'd talked more about the opportunity before she'd signed on.

"Maybe, maybe not. But if I hadn't been gone so long, we wouldn't have drifted apart."

"So are you saying you're willing to make our relationship as big a priority as your career?"

Her fingers fanned over her stomach, the gesture protective. "I think that's something we need to discuss further."

"Fair enough." He was wise enough not to hoot in delight. With her album set for release after the first of the year, he'd been worried that she'd put too much pressure on herself to start touring and take their baby away with her.

"So how can I support you better?" she asked, turning the question back on him.

He'd come prepared with answers to all the questions except this one. He didn't honestly know what he wanted from her in terms of support.

"It's pretty hard for me to rely on anyone," he said. "I'm not accustomed to asking for help."

"And yet you have a therapist you see. What do you get out of seeing her?"

"I don't have to be strong with her."

"Strong? Like confident?"

"Confident and together. I went to see her when I was struggling with depression after I realized I wasn't coming back from the Tommy John surgery. I didn't have to put on a brave face for her. I could be angry and scared and she provided a safe place for me to work through all the emotions my father told me a real man could control. He always said, 'Control your emotions, son, or they'll control you.'"

"Is that something I could do for you?"

It was hard to tell her of his fears when his every instinct insisted he appear invincible. Capable of protecting her and providing everything she and their baby could ever need. Even though she was perfectly capable of taking care of herself, he wanted to be her shelter and her strength.

"I don't know." Immediately he knew it was the wrong thing to say, yet he'd committed to being honest with her. "It goes against everything in me to let you see me as weak."

"I could never do that," she said with a startled little laugh. "You're one of the strongest men I know."

"That's exactly what I'm talking about. You see me as strong, but sometimes I'm not."

Her lips parted. She obviously intended to argue with him further, but something in his expression stopped her.

"I guess that's something else to add to the list for when we sit down with the therapist."

Kyle's lips twitched. "At this rate we're going to keep her busy for years."

The next morning, Melody showed up at his house a little after ten in the morning with coffee and bagels. Kyle was feeling groggy as he let her in. He hadn't gotten out of Club T's until nearly five. There'd been some plumbing issues in the men's bathroom that he'd stuck around to oversee.

Melody handed him a coffee. "You look tired. Rough night?"

"I don't get how Trent can do this day in and day out. I don't think I'm cut out to oversee a nightclub."

"Just party in one?"

"That's different. When I get tired I get to go home."

She laughed at him. It was good to see her infectious smile light up her eyes. Kyle resisted the urge to pull her into his arms and steal a kiss. Day six they got to have sex. He wasn't sure how Melody was feeling about it, but after not being with her for three months, he was fairly certain the anticipation was going to kill him.

But first he had to get through day five's connection exercise: forehead-to-forehead breathing for five to twenty minutes. Kyle had no idea what was supposed to happen.

"You don't look ready to do this." She headed into the kitchen and pulled his favorite cinnamon-and-sugar bagel out of the bag and began preparing it for him with slathers of honey cream cheese. "Good thing I brought sustenance."

"I'll be fine after a dose of caffeine and sugar." He noted a certain edge to his voice put there by sexual frustration. She gave him an odd glance.

"We can postpone until later."

"No." He took the plate she offered him and sat down at the breakfast bar. The moan that came out of him after his first bite made her chuckle. "I haven't had one of these in months."

"Why not?"

"Because it's something you and I do together and it's no fun without you."

His words surprised her. "You only eat bagels with me?"

"These particular bagels, yes. We found them together that morning we went for a run and you twisted your ankle."

"You carried me to the bagel place."

"We ate these." He held up the bagel, remembering how he'd kissed the loose sugar and cinnamon off her lips. "I don't think anything has ever tasted so good."

It was that moment he'd known she was the one. He'd never told her that. Nor did he speak up now. It wasn't the right time. They were starting to find each other again, but the journey was far from over.

They sat in silence eating, each lost in their own thoughts. A few minutes later he noticed her fidgeting. Did she have somewhere to go? Someone to meet? Kyle ruthlessly banished the thought.

"I think I'm awake enough to begin," he said, sliding off the barstool and holding his hand out to her. "Shall we get started?"

"The instructions said we're supposed to do this exercise for anywhere from five to twenty minutes. What do you think?"

"Being that it's our first time, I think we should try for ten minutes. Five doesn't seem to be enough and twenty seems way too long."

"You don't think you could sit still with me for twenty minutes?" She shot a mischievous glance at him from beneath her lashes.

"I'm pretty sure neither one of us is good at sitting still."

She gave up with a sigh. "You may be right."

They decided to try the exercise while sitting on the couch. Melody kicked off her shoes and took a few seconds to get comfortable. Once they were facing each other, the awkwardness kicked in. Kyle made no attempt to secure her gaze and noted that Melody was making eye contact with his shoulder.

"We're supposed to set a timer, aren't we?" she asked, pulling out her phone. "Something soothing."

"How about we end by playing one of your songs?"

"The instructions say something soothing," she murmured wryly, indicating that although she'd put her album to bed, she hadn't made peace with it. "The sound of chimes should work." She set her phone aside. "Ready?"

He nodded and they leaned forward until their foreheads touched. "Step two, synchronized breathing. Why don't you keep breathing and I'll match your rhythm."

"Does this seem like a lot of work?" she asked in a somber tone. "Like maybe we're overthinking it?"

"We're new to the process. By that I mean we haven't really taken the time to get to know each other like this." Their relationship thus far had been more like a mad dash, not a marathon they'd spent months and months training for.

"I guess." She lapsed into silence for a few seconds and breathed. Just as he was finding her rhythm, she spoke again. "Eyes open or closed?"

"It depends if you're ready to try soul gazing."

He hoped she was. This felt important to him in a way he couldn't explain. As if their failure to connect through these exercises would mean their relationship was doomed. Day three's date night had demonstrated that they continued to fail at communicating. If they couldn't connect, they couldn't communicate. At least not on the level they needed to at this time.

"Are *you* ready to try soul gazing?" she asked. Her tentative tone made him want to reassure her.

"Why don't we try eyes closed for seven synced breaths. Once we're breathing together, see how you're feeling and if you want to open your eyes."

"This New Agey side of you is so unexpected," she teased.

He gave her a playful growl. "Shut up and breathe."

Today was day six of the plan. They were supposed to have sex. Ever since Mia pointed out that this was the day they were supposed to engage in a spoiling session for her, Melody had been both excited and terrified of what was to come.

"You realize you're in charge, right?" Mia had said as they were leaving the studio and heading to their cars. "You can do as much or as little as you want."

"But I'm sure Kyle's expecting sex."

"This is a spoiling session for you. He gets his turn on day eleven." When Mia had reached her car, she opened the trunk, pulled out a tiny bag and handed it to Melody. "A little care package." The contents were wrapped in tissue. "Wait until you and Kyle are together and then open it."

"Is it like edible body paint or something?"

"It's a surprise. I think it will help."

"Thank you." Melody had given Mia a hug and headed off to her car.

Kyle had insisted on a romantic dinner before they got down to her spoiling so at least she had some time to think about what she wanted. The possibilities were endless. She could chicken out and ask him to snuggle her. She could go all in and insist they could make love. Or it could be something in between.

Every inch of her skin tingled at what was to come. Kyle never disappointed in the lovemaking arena. She was in for a fantastic evening regardless of what she chose. But it was asking for what she wanted that was the real sticking point. Why did that make her so uncomfortable?

She texted him before leaving the parking lot so when she approached the front door, it swung open and he appeared on the threshold. Even though he didn't touch her, her body went up in flames from the sheer heat of his gaze. She held out the bag Mia had given her as if something as insubstantial as brightly colored paper could act as a shield.

"What's that?" he asked, snagging the bag from her fingers as he drew her inside.

"Something Mia gave me. It's for both of us. She told me not to open it until I was with you."

"A massage oil that heats up?"

"I guessed edible body paint."

"Painting you with my fingers sounds like a wonderful idea." He brushed a kiss across her lips, leaving lingering traces of his smile behind. "I'll break out the plastic sheets."

His kiss had short-circuited her brain. How could the simple graze of his lips awaken such longing inside her? Her feet moved automatically as he guided her deeper into the house.

"Wait." She put on the brakes and stared at him. "You have plastic sheets?"

"It's Las Vegas." His eyebrows rose as if this explained everything. "They came with the place."

Melody's lips quivered into a smile. Kyle was in such high spirits that her nerves rose up once more. Could she do this? Was she ready to take this step with him? And yet, how could she not?

She wanted him so badly, but they'd rushed their relationship in the beginning, caught up in the intensity of their sexual chemistry. Was letting her body speak for how she felt the right thing to do at this stage in their reconciliation? This was only day six of their relationship revitalization—although in truth almost two weeks had passed because of all the work that had gone into meeting her album deadline.

"What's wrong?" Kyle asked, sensitive to her mood.

Screw waiting. She was only going to get more conflicted the longer she had to think about what she was doing. "Let's have sex before dinner."

Kyle stroked his knuckles over her cheek. "I'm

pretty sure that's not what you were thinking just now. Didn't we promise to do a better job of communicating?"

She held his palm to the side of her face and stared at his strong throat. Tonight he wore a long-sleeve T-shirt in dark gray that hugged his torso and hinted at the definition in his arms, chest and abs. No buttons to worry about. She could tear the thing right off him.

"I'm worried about us having sex tonight," she said at last.

He didn't tense or frown. Setting his hands on her shoulders, he gave her a gentle shake.

"So, you want to rush into something you're not ready for?" His tone was fond exasperation.

"I don't know what I want. That's part of my problem."

Kyle caressed down her arms and took her hands. His tender touch warmed her clear to her toes, banishing most of her anxiety. "This is your night." His fingers tightened on hers, offering reassurance. "We will do whatever you want."

"But you want to have sex." She wasn't trying to stir the pot and create discord, but she was sure he had expectations and wanted to be clear about them.

"I'm a guy." One corner of his lips kicked up. "I want to have sex all the time. But I don't expect you to do something because I want it. Especially not on a night when making you happy is my only goal."

Melody relaxed a little at his reassurance. More than anything this made her long to be with him.

"So, no sex before dinner." She paused. "And no sex after dinner."

He gave her a wry smile as if understanding that she was testing him. "If you weren't pregnant, I'd suggest a cocktail to relax you. Instead, I'm going to give you some sparkling cider and feed you all the delicious selections Chef Murray made for our dinner tonight."

He'd brought in a private chef who even now was in the kitchen creating an amazing array of tasting plates for them to enjoy. Kyle led her to the dining room and they took their seats. She couldn't believe her eyes; there were so many dishes to choose from.

Melody lost track of how many things she ate and couldn't decide which of the amazing dishes were her favorite. By the time the chef left them with a half-dozen desserts to sample and share, Melody's nerves were humming with pleasure.

"Time to bring out Mia's gift," she said, moaning over a flourless chocolate cake drizzled with sea salt caramel that melted in her mouth.

Kyle fetched the bag and together they pulled out a card game for lovers. Melody's first reaction was an uncomfortable giggle, but Kyle scrutinized the cards with interest.

"I think she meant well." He set them aside without further comment and rested his steady gaze upon her. "But what do you want to do next?"

Melody turned her hands palm up. "My ideas for tonight ended with the meal."

"Well, we have to do something. How about we go into the bedroom and I snuggle you for thirty minutes.

Nothing more. Clothing on," he added as if worried she might think he was pushing. "You choose whether we spoon or face each other."

This was something she could handle. "Sounds good and I want us to face each other. There's nothing I enjoy more than putting my head on your chest and listening to your heart."

"Then that's what we'll do."

Since it was her evening, Melody positioned him on his back and snuggled up next to him. With his arms around her, she settled into the deep steady rhythm of his rising and falling chest. She missed this. It was peaceful and soothing. Tight against Kyle, locked in his arms, she floated on waves of trust and love. How had she forgotten he made her feel like this? She'd been so caught up in being hurt and self-protective that the important stuff had diminished in her mind. Why was it always so easy to be negative instead of positive?

"Is something wrong?" Kyle asked. "You're not very relaxed and that was the whole point of this exercise."

"Sorry. I was thinking about how nice this is and how much I've missed it."

"And that made you tense?"

She sat up and stared down at him. Suddenly the floodgates opened and all sorts of emotions began to pour out of her.

"I'm mad at myself for shutting down instead of fighting for us. I'm frustrated that you didn't trust me." She was breathing hard now and her throat constricted to the point where she could barely speak above a whisper. "And I'm scared that if it wasn't for this baby we wouldn't be making an attempt to save our relationship."

His eyes widened at this rush of information, but he kept his voice relaxed as he said, "I think right now we need to focus on the fact that we are making an attempt to save our relationship."

"Ugh." She rolled off the bed and started pacing. "What is wrong with me that I'm so in my head?"

"There's nothing wrong with you. I'm sorry you feel like we're only trying to fix our relationship because of the baby. That's not how I feel."

"So, if I wasn't pregnant, you'd still be here fighting for us?"

"Absolutely."

He answered so quickly and with such definitiveness that the fear clutching at her heart loosened its hold. Damn it. What was she doing? The goal of days one through five was to rediscover each other and connect through talking.

Tonight was supposed to be about them reconnecting physically. Not just sex, but intimacy. She owed it to both of them to shut down her brain and indulge in some straightforward devour-each-other sex.

"Take your clothes off," she said, setting her hands on her hips and looking him over with a lover's keen eye. "Slowly." Her lips moved into a sultry grin. "Very slowly."

With a nod of understanding, Kyle got off the bed and took up a position at the foot of it. "Would you like me to dance for you as well?" He was obviously willing to give her a show.

"That would be nice." Melody went to sit cross-legged in the middle of the bed. They were too far apart to touch each other. "Do you need some music?"

Laughing with him broke down her walls. She'd put far too much emphasis on them having sex. She'd forgotten how much fun they had playing together.

"Whatever you'd like."

Melody grabbed his phone and cued up Christina Aguilera's "Still Dirrty." Kyle's eyebrows went up at her choice, but he started moving his hips to the beat. For someone who locked up his emotions, he wasn't afraid to get silly from time to time. And the man knew how to rock his body. Her mouth went dry as inch after inch of hard, sculpted muscles came into view. She could definitely get used to this.

Her fingers twitched as he slid down his zipper. She could feel the metallic rasp resonating throughout her entire body and got up on her knees as his pants hit the floor. She was eager to get her hands on the erection straining his boxer briefs. When his fingers hooked in the waistband, she stopped him.

"Wait." She smiled up at him. "Let me."

He groaned as her fingers skimmed down his stomach and dove beneath the fabric. "This is supposed to be about you."

"You don't think I enjoy touching you?" she teased, working her palm up and down his hard shaft. He pumped into her grip and slid his underwear to the floor.

"I know I enjoy having your hands on me." He gently pried her grip free. "Later," he promised. "For now we concentrate on you."

Melody stripped off her shirt and shimmied out of her leggings. Clad in bra and underwear, she scooted backward across the mattress and crooked her finger at him.

"I want you to take these off me," she said, sliding her fingers lightly over her bra and panties, delighted by the way his nostrils flared.

"And then?"

"I'd like you to touch me."

"Just touch?" He crawled up the mattress toward her. "Am I limited to hands only?"

"Of course not."

"Do you want me to take things slow?"

Did she? "Please, no. The only thing I want you to take is me. Now."

The months of separation hit her like a truck. Every inch of her ached for the caress of his hands and mouth.

He shifted to her side, fingers trailing up her thigh. When at last he brushed over the crotch of her panties and lingered over the dampness, her hips lifted off the mattress.

"That's my girl," he murmured. "Tell me what you want."

"This."

She grabbed his hand and slid it beneath the material. They groaned in mutual delight as he dragged his fingers through her wetness. His mouth found hers, the kiss hard and demanding. She opened to the thrust of his tongue and clutched at his head while he worked his fingers against her core and around her clit, the pressure perfect. The months of heartache fell away and there was only this. Always this.

"Don't hold back. Give me everything," he murmured and that was all it took.

An orgasm rushed over her so fast she was barely aware of the upsurge of pleasure before her release.

"More," she moaned against his mouth, smiling as he hooked his fingers in her panties and tugged them off her. She dispensed with her bra at the same time and then she was spread open for him. "I need you to fill me."

"We'll get there," he promised. "But first…"

Eight

She tasted like everything heavenly and memorable and the sounds she made as he spread her wide and set his tongue against her was the most beautiful music. He intended to make her come a second time, harder. Whatever it took to drive the last three months of separation from both of their minds.

"Kyle. Oh, yes, just like that."

He loved hearing her cry out his name. She would grow hoarse screaming it before he was done. He slid a finger up inside her and her hips lifted, angling to take more. He obliged her and his thrusting mimicked what would come later.

"Harder," she panted. "Make me come."

Her cries grew as he fell into the rhythm he knew she loved. She danced against his mouth. His fingers bit into her hips as he held her tight against his tongue and drove her toward orgasm. She was arching back against the mattress, her muscles flexing and straining as her pleasure rose. Gathering fistfuls of the comforter, she arched even farther back and a wordless cry spilled from her throat.

Watching her climax moved him in ways he'd never fully appreciated before. He'd done this for her. And she gave him everything.

When she went limp, he sucked in one breath and then a second. Her eyes were closed and satisfaction curved her lips. He stayed still and watched her, waited for what came next. It didn't take long.

Her lashes drifted upward. Her gaze snagged him. "Come up here." She hooked her finger at him. "I need you to kiss me."

She didn't need to tell him twice. He crawled up her body, depositing kisses as he went. He lingered over her breasts, taking one and then the other nipple into his mouth and running his tongue over the sensitive buds. Her fingers dove into his hair, holding him to her, while a stream of whimpers and cries came from her throat.

"Kiss me," she whispered.

He obliged, shifting until he loomed over her, their mouths gliding across each other in smooth, gentle strokes. His muscles began to quiver as he held himself above her. She spread her legs for him and brushed her hand down his body until she found his erection. He sucked in a sharp breath as she touched him.

"I need you inside me. Now."

"I like you being in charge," he told her, placing himself at her tight entrance, feeling the heat of her waiting for him. "Fast or slow?"

"Fast and hard. I need you to fill me. Until I'm no longer me but us."

Despite her words, he took his time, letting her adjust to their three-month absence, savoring her tight fit. She dug her fingernails into his butt, making him groan, and pulled him to her. He lost it a little on the first thrust. It had been so long. She was so perfect with her flushed skin and the indents in her lip from where she'd bitten down.

"That's it," he murmured, giving her his all, thrilled that she took him so deep and deeper still. It felt so good to be surrounded by her, body and soul. "You're incredible."

She wrapped her legs around him and he began to move. The friction amazed him. Her muscles were tight as he thrust into her, finding her rhythm and wringing a cry from her lips. He leaned down to kiss her and she gave him hunger and wildness. They rocked together harder, faster. Her nails bit into him, urging him on. *Have mercy.*

"Make me come, Kyle," she pleaded. "Again, please."

It was what he'd been waiting to hear. He gripped her ass, changed the angle of his thrusts slightly and her body tensed. He was ready to explode, but he would not let himself go until he saw her unravel again.

"Come for me," he growled, watching as her head

fell back and a wordless keening burst from her. He held himself in check for a few more thrusts and when he was sure she was over the edge, let his own orgasm claim him.

He shouted her name, a declaration to the universe that this woman belonged to him. And he to her. His chest heaved. Something hot burned in his eyes. He collapsed onto her and buried his face in her neck. Minutes ticked by as they panted in ragged, sated bliss. It was always more than just sex with Melody. It was a mind-blowing connection that couldn't be denied. Her fingers relaxed their grip on him and he shifted onto his side, drawing her with him. With their legs tangled, his fingertips stroked damp strands of hair away from her face. He dropped a kiss on her temple.

Mine.

And no one was going to take her away from him. Not ever.

Kyle was whistling as he stopped his car in Trent's driveway and slid from behind the wheel. It was six in the evening and Melody had invited him for dinner. For the first time since the day they'd attended her ultrasound appointment, they were spending time together with no purpose other than to enjoy each other's company. As much as Kyle had appreciated the exercises that had helped them reconnect and learn more about each other, he was happy to have no agenda.

After reading the note on Melody's front door, he turned in the direction of her brother's house. As much as he was looking forward to the intimate setting of the guest cottage, he understood why she was using the main house to host dinner. Trent's kitchen was three times the size of hers.

He followed the path through Trent's carefully landscaped backyard and arrived at the terrace that overlooked the swimming pool. It glowed a soft turquoise amid the cleverly lit trees and bushes that created a tropical paradise. The previous week's temperatures had hovered in the midseventies during the day, but now as December progressed, Las Vegas was seeing a nearly fifteen-degree drop. And with sunset an hour earlier than in the summer, it was downright chilly.

The scent of cooking beef lured him past the narrow opening in the sliding glass wall and into Trent's two-story great room. His friend had bought the enormous property in a gated Las Vegas community and turned it into a bachelor's playground. Before he and Melody got together, Kyle used to love to come to Vegas and hang out here. There had always been a party going on with girls and booze and plenty of distractions.

These days, although Savannah had only been back in Trent's life for a few months, the changes were evident. A playpen sat beside the large sectional. The dining room boasted a highchair. On either side of the fireplace, toys lined the bookcases' lower shelves. And below the coffee table was a basket of board books, perfect for little hands.

He imagined his own house in LA looking much the same in six months. After how things had gone between them the other night, he was pretty sure Melody was ready to move back in with him.

She stood in the kitchen, her dark brown hair pulled back in a high ponytail. She wore snug black jeans, torn at the knees, and a dark gray T-shirt that hid her baby bump. Her only jewelry, a silver guitar pick engraved with Melody + Kyle, dangled from a long chain. He'd given it to her the day she left on the tour.

Looking back, he probably should've put a large diamond on her left hand, but they'd only been living together for three months and he'd been too arrogant. He'd never imagined she'd stray during their long months apart. If anyone was prone to cheat, it probably would have been him. But being with her had changed him. Before she came along, he'd been accustomed to being alone. The minute she walked out the door, loneliness barged in and sat on his chest like an adult bull elephant.

"Something smells amazing," Kyle said, holding an enormous bouquet of pink roses and white lilies out to her. "These are for you."

Predictably, her eyes widened at the sight of so many flowers. He scanned her expression for disappointment. She probably would've preferred to receive red roses from him. But someone had already beaten him to the punch and he didn't want to remind either of them of that fact.

"These are gorgeous," she exclaimed with such delight that Kyle winced.

How long had it been since he'd showered her with tokens of his affection? He scanned his memory and realized it was too long. What was wrong with him? Melody was the most important woman in his life. She was generous, thoughtful and loving. When she'd first gone on tour, he'd taken delight in sending her little things that made her happy. But as the weeks went on and he ran out of ideas, he'd fallen back on text messages, and the romantic gifts had become less frequent.

"But you don't have to bring me flowers." She so obviously meant it that his heart contracted to the size of a peanut.

"I know you don't expect it, but that doesn't mean I should take you for granted. Hunter made that mistake and he lost you."

"That's not really why he lost me," she said quietly as she filled a vase with water and unwrapped the flowers. "I fell in love with you."

"I don't deserve you."

"Probably not." Her cheeky smile came and went. "I hope you have an appetite. I fixed your favorite."

His mouth started to water. "Beef bourguignon?"

"The very same."

It was the dish she'd fixed the night she chose him over Hunter. They'd arranged to have dinner at her apartment, not as part of the ruse, but because they both reached a point where being together—even as friends—had become the best part of their day. She confessed later that she'd created a romantic setting without even thinking about it.

He glanced toward the formal dining room and saw it was decked out with fine china, crystal glasses and flickering candles. "You went all out," he said softly, hope stirring inside him like the first glimpse of dawn.

"I thought maybe we could both use a reminder of what it was like in the beginning."

"I like that idea." His voice was a husky murmur, the best he could do given the lump in his throat. "What can I do to help?"

The fastest way to Melody's heart was to pitch in and become part of her team. She was everyone's cheerleader and preferred group sports to solo activities. It was another way they differed. He'd grown up an only child, and although he'd chosen baseball as a career because he excelled at it, pitching had always felt like one of the most isolating of positions. Often the flow of a game hinged on how well he performed. It was one thing to stand in the outfield and wait for a ball to come to you. It was another to place pitch after pitch exactly where you wanted it.

Such drive for perfection was what Kyle and Melody recognized in each other. Their disciplines might be different, but their desires sprang from the same well.

"You can open the wine," Melody said. "I pulled a lovely red from Trent's collection."

"You can't drink alcohol and I'd rather not drink alone."

She smiled sweetly and nodded. "In that case, dinner will be ready in ten minutes." She clasped her hands before her and eyed him with interest.

"How shall we entertain ourselves?" He closed the distance between them and slid his hands over her hips, drawing her gently toward him.

"Ten minutes isn't a lot of time," Melody murmured, her nails raking against his scalp in the way he liked. "And I've spent too much time cooking to let it burn."

"Then we'll just have to use the time wisely."

After dinner, they left the dishes soaking in the sink and Melody led the way to the guesthouse where she planned to offer him the dessert of his choice: a cheesecake with white chocolate and raspberry or her. As she entered the tiny living room, turning on lights as she went, she had a tiny déjà vu moment as once again Kyle spotted the basket filled with baby things she'd left on the dining room table.

"Who is that from?" He demanded.

"I don't know. There was no card." She didn't turn to look at him, afraid to see suspicion in his eyes.

"Okay." But from the tone of his voice, it wasn't okay.

"Did this get delivered to the studio as well?"

"No. It was waiting for me by my door."

He froze, eyes widening. "You are in a gated community. You didn't find that strange?"

"Um." She recalled her earlier disquiet, but didn't want to upset him. "I figured someone dropped it off with the guards and maybe they brought it by."

"But they don't have the code to the side gate. How did it get to your door?"

"It came while the crew was working on putting Christmas lights up. I figured maybe one of them brought it in."

"Did you ask them?"

"No."

The delivery method had seemed off at the time, but then she'd called Savannah and got to thinking about Kyle and their future and become completely distracted from the basket's mysterious arrival.

"Melody," he chastised, taking her by the shoulders and turning her to face him. "What the hell is going on?"

"It's not from Hunter."

Kyle's mouth drew into a grim line at the mention of her ex-boyfriend. "Did you talk to Savannah or Trent?"

"It's not from them, either." This would probably be a good time to mention how the CD from her ultrasound had gone missing as well. "There's something else."

"What?"

"Friday, after the doctor's appointment when I went to show Mia the ultrasound, it wasn't in my purse."

"You lost it?"

"I looked all over the studio and asked around but nobody had seen it. And then two days later it was back in my purse. I swear it wasn't there on Friday when I wanted to show it to Mia."

"Do you think someone at the studio took it and then gave it back?"

"No. Why would anyone do that? I just figured maybe it had fallen out and someone found it and put it back. The CD has my name on it."

"This is really strange and I'm not sure it's a good idea for you to stay here alone."

Kyle's concern was causing her anxiety to spike,

but she pulled it under control. "Don't be ridiculous. Like you said, this is a gated community. It's all just a coincidence."

"I don't believe in coincidences. There's something weird going on and I don't like the idea of you staying here by yourself."

"I'm fine."

"Humor me."

"Humor you how?"

"Move into my place." He must've picked up on her dismay, because he quickly added, "At least while Trent and Savannah are gone."

"That's not necessary, I assure you."

But the basket's mysterious origin couldn't be denied. She put on a brave face, not wanting Kyle to think she was feeling even the littlest bit anxious. Red roses and baby gifts weren't exactly frightening, no matter what the source.

"I don't like that someone has such easy access to you."

"So I'll call the guard at the gate and let them know that no deliveries for this address should be allowed past them. And then I'll talk to Trent and make sure he doesn't have any more landscaping projects planned."

Kyle didn't appear satisfied with her answer. He crossed his arms and frowned down at her. "Then I'm going to move in here."

"Definitely not. We are not ready to cohabit again."

"I'm not talking about cohabitation, I'm talking about your safety."

"Roses and bibs. Not exactly scary stuff."

"Anonymous gifts."

"So I have a secret admirer," she said flippantly. It took a second for her own words to sink in. The reality of a secret admirer wasn't nearly as delightful as it sounded. "I'm sure it's harmless."

The skeptical expression on Kyle's face matched his words. "You need to take this more seriously. You're in the public eye now. People think they know you. They believe they have a personal connection even though they've never met you."

He'd had his own experiences with such fans. There was the woman who'd posed as his girlfriend and bluffed her way into his hotel room not once, but twice, while he was on the road with the team. Later, she'd bombarded him with letters and presents, making quite a nuisance of herself. Eventually he'd had to get a restraining order against her. Still, she'd threatened to commit suicide in an LA boutique after she spotted him shopping there with a woman he was seeing.

"I'm not famous in the same way you are," Melody said. "I'm just that girl who opened for Free Fall. I don't have a big following on Twitter or Instagram. Maybe once my album drops it will be different."

"It only takes one person."

Kyle wasn't the sort of guy to try to frighten her just so he could persuade her to move in with him. If he was alarmed, he was genuinely concerned about her.

"Okay, now you're scaring me," she said.

"Good."

"Can you give me tonight to think about it?"

Kyle began sifting through the baby items; she

couldn't imagine what he was looking for. The last thing he picked up was the teddy bear. As he turned it over in his hands, he began to frown.

"There's something weird about this." He fiddled with it some more and produced a black box from the back of it. He looked shaken, and alarms started going off in her head.

"What's wrong?"

"This is a camera. One of the teddy bear's eyes is the lens."

"A what?" She glanced around her living room, trying to imagine the space from the angle of the stuffed toy. "You mean like one of those nanny cams?"

"Yes."

He regarded the thing with a frown before walking it outside. She followed him as far as the door and watched as he dropped it into the pool. Her skin felt as if it was crawling with a hundred tiny insects. She shuddered and set her hand against her lips as her stomach roiled.

"I don't know what's going on," he said, returning to the guesthouse. "But I don't like it one bit. You can't stay here a second longer."

He had her good and spooked. Suddenly, the idea of an alarm system between her and the rest of the world sounded pretty great. She half wished Savannah and Trent had left Murphy behind. The French bulldog might not be big enough to take down the intruder, but he was fierce enough to bark and warn her if anyone was trying to get in.

The main house had an alarm system and no creepy,

anonymous gifts sitting on the dining room table. "What if I go sleep in Trent's extra bedroom? There's an alarm system and I know no one has been inside. Let me pack a bag and you can walk me over."

"It would be better if you didn't stay alone."

"I'll be fine."

Whatever she'd intended for the evening was now spoiled by her fear of stalkers. While Kyle stood in her living room like a guard dog on high alert, she threw stuff that she'd need into an overnight bag. Her nerves jangled as she stared around her bedroom, seeing the big windows and the drapes she never drew. What would be the point? There was an eight-foot wall around the perimeter of Trent's large backyard. She'd never imagined a stranger would be peering in her windows.

After locking up, she and Kyle returned to the main house and he made the rounds, checking each window and door to make sure it was locked. Melody wore a frustrated frown through this process, but it was mostly to hide her anxiety. She'd planned for such a different end to the evening.

She should ask Kyle to stay, but she'd made such a big deal out of not needing him. She'd asserted that she wasn't ready to resume their relationship so many times that she wasn't sure how to stop pushing him away. What was it going to take for her to give up and give in? If a stalker wasn't the perfect excuse to admit she needed and wanted to rely on Kyle once again, then what would it take?

"Everything seems to be secure," Kyle said, standing in the middle of the great room and staring around.

Melody wrapped her fingers around his arm and nudged him toward the front door. "I'll be fine."

Part of her wanted to take him up to the guest room and tear off his clothes, but it was an impulse born of anxiety and fear of being alone. That wouldn't do. It wasn't fair to either of them. And how long before this real or imagined threat stopped being an excuse for her to turn to him?

Feeling proud of herself for being so sensible, Melody lifted onto her tiptoes, wrapped her arms around his neck and gave him a chaste kiss before sending him out the door.

Nine

As soon as Kyle heard the front door lock click into place behind him, he pulled out his phone and dialed Trent. When his friend answered, Kyle heard a shrieking baby and a barking dog in the background.

"Sounds like a party at your house," Kyle said. Opening his car door, he slid behind the wheel, but didn't start the engine. All at once he realized he couldn't bring himself to leave Melody by herself. He would spend the night in his car out in front of the house. There was no way anyone was getting past him.

"Dylan stole Murphy's favorite toy and thinks it's funny when he gets barked at."

Despite the concern weighing him down, Kyle couldn't help smiling. Was that chaos going to be his life a year from now or was it different having a girl? He couldn't wait to find out.

"So what's up?" Trent asked. "Something going on at the club?"

"Everything is running as smoothly as it can. I'm calling about your sister."

"I'd like to help you, but Melody's got a mind of her own."

"Don't I know it." Kyle rubbed his forehead. "But this isn't about playing go-between in our relationship. It's something more serious."

"I don't think I like the sound of that."

Kyle suspected Melody wouldn't be happy with him for calling her brother, but she wasn't taking this situation seriously enough. "Some weird stuff has been happening to her."

"Define weird."

"I think she's called you or Savannah about some flowers that got delivered to the studio."

"Red roses. Yes, Savannah mentioned something about it. You didn't send them, I take it?"

"No, and she's convinced that Hunter didn't, either."

"You believe her?" Trent sounded relieved and worried at the same time.

"I like to think I've learned a little something these last few months."

Trent snorted. "Yeah, you keep telling yourself that."

"Fine, I'm a jealous fool." And for the first time in three months, it didn't make him feel bad. Because it meant he cared. He felt. A lot. "Your sister is important to me. That's why I've been acting like such an idiot."

"You remember what I said to you when you first started dating her? I said I'd kick your ass if you hurt her. You promised me you wouldn't."

"I'm not overjoyed at the detour our conversation has taken. It's never been my intention to hurt your sister."

"I figured you were both adults and she knew what she was getting with you." For some reason Trent was on a roll. "Frankly, I thought you'd move on before she got too attached."

"I'm committed to making a life with Melody and our child. Nothing about that has changed. She's the one with questions and doubts." By the time Kyle got all that out, he was working hard to get air in and out of his tight chest. "Now, can we please get back to the anonymous gifts she's been getting."

"What else has arrived?"

"A basket of baby things."

"Savannah mentioned something about that. You didn't send it?"

Kyle wished he had. "No. And it showed up on her doorstep. No card. Nothing at all to indicate who it came from."

"What do you mean it showed up on her doorstep?"

"I mean someone got into your gated community and into your locked backyard and put it on the front step of the guesthouse."

"How the hell did that happen?"

That was the same question Kyle wanted answers

to. His uneasiness grew with Trent's concern added to the mix.

"I don't know. I had her move into your house for tonight because there's an alarm. It's a start, but I would feel even more confident of her safety with her at my place. She, however, is resisting."

"Do a better job of convincing her."

Kyle resisted snapping at his best friend. None of this was Trent's fault. Taking a few seconds to gather and then expel a long, steadying breath, Kyle said, "That's my plan, but your sister has a mind of her own." Thank goodness. And yet with her safety at risk, Kyle wished she was a little bit more tractable.

"What do you want me to do?"

"I don't suppose you could come up with a good reason for her to come to LA for a visit?"

"I know Nate's been talking about her doing a concert to kick off her album. Maybe we could put something together here."

"Do you want to give him a call?" Kyle asked. "Or should I?"

"I'll do it. What are you planning for the rest of the night?"

"I thought I'd sit in my car and watch your house."

A long pause followed his words. When Trent spoke, he sounded more serious than ever. "Is that really necessary?"

"Maybe not, but she and the baby are the two most important people in my world. I can't risk anything happening to either of them. And it's not as if I'm going to be able to go home and sleep."

"I'll call Nate and let you know what I find out."

Kyle pushed back his seat and settled in for a long night. At least he wasn't going to struggle to stay awake. His nerves were too much on edge to allow him to sleep. With his phone connected to Trent's Wi-Fi, the car filled with live sports talk from *ESPN*. The conversation didn't do much to tax his attention, but the sound kept him alert. An hour into his vigil, Trent called back.

"My sister called to tell me there's a stalker in her driveway." Trent's drawl lacked any tension, so he obviously knew where Kyle was at the moment. "Any idea who that might be?"

"Text her back and let her know that come morning I expect coffee and some of those disgusting frozen waffles you keep in your freezer."

"She says you should come in."

"She wasn't too happy about the idea earlier." Kyle knew he was being stubborn, but he had a point to make and she'd started it. "I'm fine right here."

"Suit yourself. I talked to Nate and he agrees about you taking her to LA for a while."

"Great." A weight was already lifting off Kyle's shoulders. "Now all we have to do is come up with a reasonable explanation for her to go."

"Already in motion."

Dawn was pushing salmon and gold into the sky when Kyle heard a knock on his car window. He'd been staring toward the street and didn't notice Melody approaching from the house. He rolled down the window.

"I thought you would've given up and gone home

by now," she said, setting her hands on the door and leaning down. "You look like hell."

"Good morning, gorgeous," he murmured, surveying her messy updo, the sleepy droop of her lips and the hint of cleavage peeking out between the sagging lapels of her robe. "Sleep well?"

"Not particularly." She gave him no more explanation. "Hungry?"

"Sure."

"Come on in. I fixed breakfast."

"Coffee and waffles?"

"You hate those waffles."

"I didn't figure there was anything else available."

"You forget Trent doesn't live alone anymore. Savannah makes sure the freezer and refrigerator are well stocked. There's bacon, eggs and toast. As well as coffee."

"You didn't have to go to all that trouble."

She gave him an unreadable look before pushing away from the car. "Come get it while it's hot."

Kyle followed her inside, gleefully sucking in the invigorating aroma of coffee and bacon. Instead of eating at the breakfast bar, they brought their plates to the couch in Trent's great room and sat side by side.

Twenty minutes later, Kyle set his finished plate on the coffee table and sat back with a groan. "That was fantastic," he said, glancing her way. "Are you sure you got enough to eat?"

"I'm just starting to get my appetite back so I had plenty." She carried their plates to the kitchen.

"Here, let me help."

Together they rinsed the dishes and pans before loading the dishwasher. They worked in companionable silence while the morning television show updated them on the latest news. Despite her attempt to maintain her outward calm, Melody buzzed with nervous energy.

"I spent a lot of time thinking last night and I really do believe this is all just a huge overreaction." From the rock-solid set of her jaw, she'd obviously decided to go on as if there was no threat.

Kyle was not on board with this. "Feel like heading to LA for a week or so with me?" Maybe once he got her back to LA and into his house, she'd feel inclined to stay there.

"Aren't you supposed to be minding the store while Trent is gone?"

"Nate can take over for a little while."

She leaned back against the counter and crossed her arms. "I suppose if I don't you'll be spending every night in the driveway?"

"It's a possibility." More likely he'd hire a security guy to watch over her.

"I think the neighbors will start to get concerned."

"Yes," he drawled. "Let's worry about what the neighbors think."

She made a face at him. "The thing is, how long do I live like this? Fearing things that may or may not be real?"

Kyle considered. Her point was valid. He hated the idea that she would be looking over her shoulder until she moved back to LA. And he was assuming that was where they were going to end up. On the other hand, he wasn't all that keen on her anonymous gift giver escalating to more personal contact.

"Let's go…" He barely stopped himself from saying *home*. "Get some shopping done for the baby at those ridiculously expensive Rodeo Drive stores and hang out at the beach."

When she immediately agreed, Kyle was a little surprised at her change of heart. Then, he decided it was less about her interest in buying baby stuff and more about getting away from a scary situation. But either way he thought, as he folded her into his arms, he'd take the win.

A couple days after Kyle spent the night in his car outside Trent's house, Melody found herself the victim of some clever manipulations on the part of her brother, Nate and Kyle.

"I'm giving a concert at The Roxy?" She was sitting in Nate's office at Ugly Trout Records. Her emotions whirled in a combination of excitement and trepidation. "When?"

"A little over a week."

"How am I supposed to do that?" The band that had backed her up on the Free Fall tour had all gone off to new gigs. She had no idea what to sing. "I can't be ready to perform that fast."

"It's all set. I've hired the musicians, and they already have the arrangements of your songs. I also leased the practice space. You just need to show up in LA and rehearse."

She crossed her arms over her chest. "Seems like you've thought of everything. Whose idea was this?"

"Several people provided input."

"This is your way of getting me out of Las Vegas and away from my supposed stalker." Melody blew out a breath. "Nothing weird has happened since the basket arrived. We don't even know that there is a stalker."

"A performance at The Roxy is still a great idea."

"You're right. I've got a lot to do. When do Kyle and I leave for LA?"

"How'd you know Kyle was going with you?"

"Because he's become my watchdog for the last three days."

After he'd spent the night in Trent's driveway, it became apparent that Kyle wasn't going to be happy unless he could keep an eye on her so she'd agreed to move into his guest room. They still weren't in a place where she was ready to go back to their former arrangement, but being compelled to spend more time together had sped up the relationship revitalization process.

"You leave the day after tomorrow. That'll give you a week to rehearse."

"It's tight." But she knew a lot more about getting ready for a performance after spending so many months on tour. "But doable."

After leaving Nate's office, Melody went in search of Mia and found the songwriter working beside Craig in studio C's control booth. A few weeks earlier, Nate had brought Mia under his wing and was training her to produce music. The industry was dominated by men and Melody was delighted her friend was doing her part to change that.

When Mia looked over and spotted Melody entering, her eyes lit up. "So? Are you excited?"

"Very. And a little nervous. I've got a lot to do in a short period of time."

"You'll be great."

Craig took his eyes off the studio musicians going to town on the other side of the glass and observed her with interest. "What's up?"

"I'm going to be performing at The Roxy in a week."

Now it was his turn to grin. "That's great. You'll be fantastic."

"I hope so." Melody soaked up her friends' encouragement as she took a seat next to Mia. "It was really nice of Nate and Trent to organize this for me."

"I think you can use a break from Las Vegas," Mia said, her eyes saying more than her words.

They'd all decided to keep quiet about her stalker. As much as Nate trusted his staff, there were all sorts of people coming and going in the studio. It wouldn't do for word to get out. And Melody couldn't forget that the roses had been delivered here and the business with the CD of her ultrasound vanishing and reappearing had taken place in the studio, too.

"It will be good to go…" She'd been about to say home. "Get away."

"How long do you think you'll stay?" Mia asked.

Craig had returned his attention to the musicians, leaving the women to their conversation.

"I'm not sure. It depends on how things go." She stared at her fingers for a second before adding, "Kyle wants us to spend Christmas together in LA."

"How do you feel about that?"

"I'd rather be with family."

"But he's your family, too," Mia reminded her.

"Yes, but I don't want to have to choose between you all and him."

Mia eyed her sympathetically. "I understand how you feel. Ivy didn't exactly make it easy for me when Nate and I were trying to sort out our relationship." Not only were Mia and Ivy twins, but Mia had been Ivy's constant companion ever since the pop star had started her career at age six. She'd even been her personal assistant once they were older.

"But in the end, you chose Nate because you loved him."

"And you'll choose Kyle for the same reasons."

Melody nodded, even as she hoped that when the time came, Mia would be right.

It was day eight, another date night. Melody wanted to do something upbeat and fun after the emotionally exhausting discussion they'd had during the prior day's exercise.

Day seven had been about communicating. Each person was supposed to take twenty minutes to talk uninterrupted about whatever was on their mind. Melody had spoken about her upcoming booking at The Roxy, sharing her excitement and fears about the solo show and how her new songs would be received.

Kyle had spoken about his father, sharing a story about how he'd canceled Kyle's tenth birthday party at the last minute after his baseball team had lost in the final inning of the playoffs. Kyle had missed catching a fly ball and the other team had scored. Kyle's father had declared only winners got to have a party.

Melody's heart had broken while Kyle told his story. She wanted to call his father and scold him on Kyle's behalf, but she knew it would do no good. Kyle's father wasn't going to apologize to his son for such misguided treatment because he thought he was teaching Kyle a life lesson by being so hard on him. Instead, she'd put her arms around Kyle and let him know she'd heard his pain.

The exchanges had brought them to a place of intimacy they hadn't achieved before and filled Melody with confidence for their future.

For their eighth date, they were supposed to take a class in something that neither of them had done. Melody had been thinking about this for a while and decided she'd come up with an idea that would provide the sort of team spirit they were trying to achieve.

"I want to learn how to tango," Melody said.

Ever since Kyle had treated her to an evening of sexual spoiling, she'd been feeling an increase in her libido. She wasn't sure if it had something to do with the easing of her nausea, the second trimester hormones kicking in, or her album being done at last, but she'd become obsessed with getting her hands on Kyle as often as she could.

"Tango?" He looked more intrigued than resistant.

"It always looks so sexy when people do it on TV."

He laughed. "I'm sure they've had tons of practice. But I'm game. If nothing else the class will be loads of fun."

This was something else she could add to her growing list of things she appreciated about him. He was always ready to take on new challenges. Even ones that pushed him out of his comfort zone.

"I found someone who will give us a private lesson tonight at seven."

"Dinner first or afterward?"

"First, I think." She gave him a wicked smile. "I'm hoping tangling on the dance floor will prompt us to want to tangle in the sheets."

"I'm all in."

Melody was surprised how slowly the rest of the day went. They had a quick dinner at what was becoming their favorite Las Vegas restaurant, a small Italian place with great food. Melody barely tasted her lasagna and when they arrived at the small dance studio, she was practically vibrating with anticipation.

"So you two want to learn the tango." Their instructor, Juliet, was a lithe blonde with the straight spine of a ballroom dancer. "Is it for your wedding?"

"No," Melody answered, glancing at Kyle.

"Tonight it's just for fun." He met her gaze. His eyes contained a somber note at odds with the half smile curving his lips.

It was at that moment that she realized he really did want to marry her. Not because of the baby, or not *only* because of the baby. He wanted them to be together.

So did she. And the way things had been going with this relationship revitalization exercise, they might actually make it.

To her surprise, butterflies took flight in her stomach when Kyle caught her hand and led her onto the dance floor. He moved with confidence, following Juliet's instructions, and slid his hand onto Melody's back. They stood facing each other, the upper halves of their bodies touching.

"Okay, let's begin," Juliet said. "Kyle, you are going to step forward with your left, forward with your right, forward with your left and to the side with your right, sliding your left foot as you go."

She demonstrated his steps and then Melody's, before slowly calling out the movement as they imitated what she'd shown them. To everyone's surprise they managed the four steps without mishap.

"Very nice," Juliet said. "Let's practice that a few more times and then move on. Remember to bend your knees as you move and keep your spine straight."

Melody found the experience to be both frustrating and exhilarating. At times her feet didn't go where they were supposed to and she lost her frame when she started thinking too much. Kyle, on the other hand, was a rock. He moved with careful deliberation through each step. His hold on her didn't waver and she learned confidence in the circle of his strong arms.

"You've done this before," the instructor said to him as they approached the end of their lesson.

"Never the tango," Kyle said. "And I haven't danced in a long time."

"How long?" Melody asked, curious at his unexpected talent.

"When I was a kid, my mom put me in dance lessons. From age six to eight I learned how to ballroom dance. I didn't exactly hate it, but it sure wasn't what my friends were doing. She thought it would be a safer activity for me than playing baseball."

"What made you stop?"

"Believe it or not my dad didn't know what I was up to and when he found out, he forced my mom to stop sending me to classes. He enrolled me in baseball instead."

How could a father not know what his son was up to for two years? Melody wanted to ask, but Juliet started the music once again and they took their places to go over the steps they'd learned one final time before the session was over.

"You must come back and dance more," Juliet said. "You are both fine students."

Kyle's fingers tightened around Melody's. "I'd be open to it if you would."

"It would be fun. This has been a great experience." She felt closer to Kyle. Something about having to coordinate their steps had put them in sync. It was a little bit like the breathing exercise they had done on day five.

"It was a great suggestion," Kyle said as they headed out to the parking lot.

"At first I wondered why you were so willing to go along with me. Now I find out you took dance lessons as a kid."

"It's not exactly something that ups my rep as a cool guy."

"No, but it does up your rep as a sexy guy." She put her arm around his waist and snuggled close. "And the way you can move your hips gets me thinking that maybe we should go back to the house and do some more dancing."

"I like the way your mind works."

Ten

With rehearsals done for the day, Melody entered the Bird Streets house she'd shared with Kyle for three short months. At first it had felt a little strange to be back in LA and staying with him in the place where once she'd been so wildly optimistic. When she'd first moved in, they'd seemed to be in sync and she'd pinned her hopes on an idyllic future with him. But as the months went on and she'd grown frustrated with his unwillingness or inability to tell her how he felt, she'd become afraid of being hurt. Afraid that he'd disappoint her the way her father and Hunter had.

But in the past week, as she'd split her attention between preparing for her concert at The Roxy and the daily exercises that were bringing her and Kyle closer together, she'd been noticing a shift in her perspective.

Each day it was a little easier to open up to Kyle and although conversations about the future continued to make Melody anxious, they'd recently had a wonderful evening stargazing and spent a day showing their appreciation for each other with love notes and special surprises.

Today they were supposed to have sex. This time, it was Kyle's turn to be spoiled. Melody was ready for this. She had no problem with anything he wanted to do. Their physical relationship had always been comfortable. Much more so than their emotional one.

She found him in the great room with its tall ceilings, movable wall of windows and fantastic views of downtown LA. He was sitting on a barstool, staring out at the pool. His laptop was on the breakfast bar nearby, its screen saver engaged. How long had he been sitting here staring off into space?

"So what's it gonna be?" she asked, stepping into his line of sight. Setting her hands on her hips, she walked toward him with a sultry swagger. "I'm yours to command."

"I'm not really feeling it today."

Seeing him shut down after everything they'd been through these last couple weeks worried her, but she refused to let him see her concern. "Oh, no," she said, setting her fingertip against his chest and pressing just hard enough to drive her point home. "It's my day to spoil you. We're having sex. That's all there is to it."

"Fine," he grumbled, crossing his arms over his chest.

"That's the attitude." For some reason his annoyance sparked her libido. "It's your day. What do you want me to do?"

He scowled at her. "I suppose you could start by taking your clothes off."

His grumpiness flowed off her like water cascading over a well-waxed car. "Do you want me to just get naked or do you want a show?"

Her words got through to him because his eyes flared briefly before narrowing.

"What sort of a show?"

"I'm yours to command." To further unsettle him, she put her palms together and bowed her head. "How may I be of service?"

When she peered up at him, he was regarding her in helpless amusement. At last she'd gotten through to him. To further tickle his funny bone, she gave him a silly little shimmy of her shoulders, her version of the burlesque dancers of old. And then, inspiration struck. She began to sing.

She strutted around the room, dropping her T-shirt off her shoulder in a parody of seduction as she sang "Let Me Entertain You."

It was working. His lips were twitching uncontrollably. She grabbed a pillow off the white sectional, put her back to him and stripped off her top.

Setting the pillow against her chest, she turned and faced him. One at a time she slid her bra straps down her arm as she kept singing with an exaggerated swagger.

The gleam in his eyes gave her the encouragement she needed to pop the clasp on her bra and slip the thing from her body. She twirled it around her finger a few times before launching it in his direction. He caught it and draped it over his shoulder.

"If the album tanks," she said with a sassy grin. "I may audition for a burlesque show."

"I'll be in the front row opening night."

She beamed at him. "'I'm very versatile.'"

Once again she turned her back to him. This time she held the pillow out from her chest while she unbuttoned her pants one-handed. She spun, grabbed a second pillow, spun, held the second pillow over her backside while she awkwardly skimmed out of her pants and then with a laugh turned to face him holding both pillows over her body.

"That was quite complicated," she said, breathing hard from her exertions.

"You did a great job."

She did a great bump and grind all the way to his chair. When she was standing before him, wearing a big smile and a couple of pillows, she finished her song.

Then she tossed the pillows to either side and threw her arms around him. Her lips found his and a second later his hands coasted over her skin. He got to his feet, fingers sliding beneath the elastic of her underwear. Cupping her bare bottom, he lifted her against his erection.

She moaned and scraped her nails against his scalp. She opened for him and his tongue swept in to devour her. The kiss started hot and became incendiary as he skimmed her underwear down her thighs and lifted her into the air. She wrapped her thighs around his waist and let him carry her to the bedroom.

He lowered her to the bed and quickly stripped off his clothes. Even though tonight was about spoiling him, she took pleasure in his beautiful, powerful body bared to her greedy gaze.

Naked. Aroused. Male. It just didn't get better than this. Color darkened his cheekbones as he set his knee on the bed and came toward her.

"Tonight is all about you," she reminded him.

Her fingers ached to touch him, so she reached out and smoothed her palm down his chest, over his washboard abs, before clasping him in a firm grip. He sucked in a breath through clenched teeth. Now that she had his full attention, she gazed up at him.

"What would you like me to do?" She hadn't intended to pitch the question so seductively, but her own aroused state gave her voice a husky purr.

Kyle hesitated, seeming to fight for the words. They'd always been very good at giving each other pleasure, each sensing what the other would like without having to be told. But their goal with the relationship revitalization project was to learn to communicate and she intended for him to tell her what he wanted.

"Your wish is my command," she prompted.

His lashes lowered and he watched her through half-slit eyes. "I'd very much like to have your mouth on me."

"Of course." She'd expected this and didn't need much encouragement. "Can you point to a specific spot?"

He looked positively grim as he pointed to his cheek. She gave him a sweet peck before looking up at him with wide-eyed curiosity. Next, he drew his finger down his neck to the base of his throat. She obliged him by trailing her lips to the spot where his pulse throbbed. Nipping at his skin rewarded her with a surprised exhalation.

She wondered how long he'd last at this game. He surprised her by taking her lips on a tour of his entire torso before arriving at the destination they were both eager to reach. She took him into her mouth, loving the silky texture of him, his salty taste and the deep, long groan that rumbled from his chest as she rolled her tongue around and over him.

Without knowing what else he wanted from her, she settled in to make him crazy. With tongue, lips and hands she worked him to the edge of orgasm and held him there. Occupied as she was, she had no way of asking him what was next. It was up to him to tell her.

His fingers bit into her upper arms, drawing her attention. "Not like this. Not tonight. I want to come inside you."

That's all she needed to hear. Shifting position, she kissed her way up his body until she straddled him. Judging from the intense light in his eye, he'd had enough of her taking care of him. Now, he reached between their bodies, positioned himself and drove into her. The feel of him filling her was a joy she could never get enough of. His hands on her hips told her the rhythm he wanted. Guiding her into a fast, steady pace, Melody found her herself rushing toward her climax sooner than she'd expected.

"Come for me," Kyle said to her. "I want to watch."

Melody pumped her hips, increasing her pleasure. Knowing he loved it when she touched herself, she slipped her hands over her breasts and played with her nipples. His hoarse curse made her smile. A second later, her head fell back as her orgasm claimed her. Kyle's fingers bit into her hips as he pumped almost frantically into her. She rode him to a second climax, and cried out his name.

"Yes," he rasped, his heart thudding wildly beneath her palm. "That's my girl."

She was his. In that moment of perfect clarity she recognized he'd own her heart forever. Was that why she'd been so afraid? Why she'd kept her distance? Because she belonged to him and that didn't seem fair when she couldn't claim his heart as hers?

Distantly, she heard his shout of release and her own name pouring from his lips as he came inside her with a final deep thrust. His fingers bit into her skin as if he was trying to make them one body instead of two. She gazed down at him, watched as unfettered joy replaced concentration on his strong features.

Chest heaving, he opened his eyes and the look there stole her breath. He gave her everything in that single moment of contact, of connection. But as she held her breath, waiting for the words to come, he only cupped her face between his palms and brought her head down for a sweetly sensual kiss.

"No woman has ever made me feel the way you do."

It wasn't *I love you*, but she'd take it. What choice did she have? She'd given him her heart and had to trust that he would take good care of it.

"I love you," she murmured and sighed as his arms tightened around her.

The afternoon of her performance, Melody headed to The Roxy for her sound check. Kyle had offered to come with her, but she was in such a state of anxiety over her first solo concert that she turned him down. She'd rather have him see her in her element tonight instead of having him witness the meltdown she could feel brewing.

She needn't have worried. The group of musicians backing her up were professional and fantastic to work with.

As she and the band were finishing up an hour before the doors opened, Hunter strolled in. She was surprised to see him and as the stage cleared, she sat down on the edge with her feet dangling.

"What are you doing here?" she asked.

"Nate mentioned you were performing tonight so I asked if I could introduce you. I thought you could use all the support you could get."

"That's really nice of you." Her stomach knotted as she wondered how Kyle would feel about seeing him here.

"I hear congratulations are in order," Hunter said. "Nate told me that you and Kyle are back together."

"I guess we are." Things between them had been going pretty fantastic this week. Being in LA had brought back all the great times they'd had together and Kyle had gone out of his way to make her feel special and adored.

"You don't sound sure." Hunter came to stand before her, one hand resting on the stage on either side of her hips, not quite touching, but suggestive all the same.

"It's been a challenging few months since you and I were in New York that night." In all the weeks that they'd worked together at Ugly Trout, Melody had kept things as far away from personal topics as she could. But for some reason, now that she felt more secure in her relationship with Kyle, she wanted some answers. "He has this crazy idea that you want to get me back." She wanted to hear him deny it.

"It's not so crazy." He took her hands and gave a gentle squeeze. "You know I'll always be there for you, right?"

She didn't know that, but nodded anyway. Kyle's words came back to haunt her. Hunter couldn't possibly want her back. But staring into his eyes, she could understand why Kyle was so insistent. The vibe rolling off Hunter reminded her of how she'd once felt so desperate to be loved by him.

"I feel the same way about you." She pulled her hands free and forced a smile to her lips. "But Kyle is my future. We're going to be a family." And after this past week, she was really starting to believe it.

"You have a full house out there," Nate said, popping into her dressing room shortly before she was to go on.

"I don't know why I'm nervous." Melody puffed out a breath and shook her hands to ease the tension in her muscles. She couldn't go out on stage looking like a wooden soldier.

At least it wouldn't last long. She was always besieged by preshow jitters. Yet, as soon as she stepped onto the stage, all her doubts faded away. It became about the music and the lyrics.

He gave her a quick, fierce hug and then smiled down at her. "You're going to do great."

"Thanks."

Together they walked through the backstage area. Out on stage, the group of musicians she'd been rehearsing with for the past week settled in while Hunter warmed up the crowd. Melody focused on the people in the audience who would be rooting for her with everything they had. Kyle, Nate, Mia, Trent and Savannah. She would sing for them.

And then Hunter was gesturing in her direction and Melody stepped on stage. She smiled and waved as if her stomach wasn't doing cartwheels and stepped up to the mic.

"Hey, LA, how is everybody doing tonight?"

The crowd came back to her with an enthusiastic howl that made all Melody's problems fade into the background. She started the first of her planned ten songs, reassured when her voice sounded strong and pure, unaffected by the anxiety attacking her nerves and making her hands shake. During the nine months on tour, she'd faced thousands of fans in huge arenas. They'd been a faceless sea, undulating as they'd danced to her music.

Tonight's crowd was different. She could feel their energy surrounding her, inspiring her performance. The intimacy thrilled her. She connected with them, recognized familiar faces. They were here for her. She wasn't an anonymous opening act for Free Fall, she was Melody Caldwell, rising star.

As she came off the stage, it seemed as if her feet barely touched the ground. If she'd been worried about how her new album would go over, tonight's crowd set her mind at ease. They'd been wonderfully receptive to every song. And she'd poured her heart and soul into every note.

"You were fantastic," Hunter called over the wild cheering.

To Melody's surprise he caught her up into his arms and spun her around. The shadows of doubt and fear creeping over her these last few weeks had been burned away by the strength of the spotlight. She laughed and hugged him back, glad he was there to share the moment with her.

Hunter set her back on her feet. And then suddenly his lips were on hers. For a second she was too surprised to move. In the back of her mind Melody recognized that this was New York City all over again. A different club. A completely innocent moment between friends. Utterly open to misinterpretation. A heartbeat too slow, she pulled back and broke the kiss.

"What the hell do you think you're doing?" she demanded, her delight crushed by Hunter's actions.

Hunter gave no sign that her distress registered on him. "Do you have one more song?" he asked eagerly, motioning toward the wave of sound rolling in from the audience. "They seem to want more."

It was then she noticed the trio that stood less than ten feet away. From the expression on Savannah's face, it was pretty obvious they had seen her embracing Hunter. Trent looked surprised, but it was Kyle's stiffness and the betrayal lurking in his gaze that told her she'd screwed up again.

"Not one the band knows," she said. "But I have a song I can do with just the keyboard."

Turning her back on Hunter, she stepped back onto the stage. With a tentative wave at the audience, she approached the keyboard player.

"Can I borrow this for a song?" She asked over the cheering crowd, her gaze straying backstage in search of Kyle.

"Be my guest."

She adjusted the keyboard mic and smiled at the crowd. "This is a little something that I've been working on with a very talented songwriter friend of mine, Mia Navarro. I hope you like it."

The crowd quieted and she began the first bars of the song. It was something near and dear to both women, a song of love and longing. Of hope and fear. Written during a time when neither believed they could ever be with the men they loved. Melody cracked her heart wide open and sang with everything she had. What poured out was vulnerable and poignant and as she finished the last note, the room was utterly silent.

A tear slid down her cheek and she brushed it away. The room erupted.

As she bowed and waved at the audience, grateful for the outpouring of love and approval, she cast glances toward the wings. She'd sung for the man standing backstage. The lights blinded her and she couldn't see past Trent and Savannah to where she assumed Kyle was standing in shadow.

Instincts told her to get to him as soon as possible, but she had an obligation to her fans as well. At long last, she could resist the pull no longer and made her way offstage. This time, instead of rushing to Hunter, she went past him, eyes darting around the people gathered to congratulate her.

First Savannah and then Trent hugged her. Their trio was joined by Nate and Mia, but when Melody looked around for Kyle, she didn't see him.

With her heart crushed by disappointment, Melody fought back tears and tried to appear normal. She gave Mia a questioning look. "Was it okay that I played our song?"

"Okay?" Mia's eyes were overly bright. "It was fantastic. As many times as I've heard my sister sing one of my songs, it was always spoiled by the fact that she was taking credit. You are the first artist to sing a Mia Navarro song. And you killed it."

"I might've been the first, but I'm not going to be the last."

As the group made their way back into the club for a celebratory drink, Melody slipped up beside Savannah and leaned close. "What happened to Kyle?"

"He said he had to make a call." Savannah linked her arm through Melody's. Her reassuring smile wasn't having the right effect.

"He saw me with Hunter, didn't he?"

"Yeah." Savannah drew the word out, obviously reluctant to put a damper on the evening. "He didn't look happy when he left."

"I've screwed up again. What is wrong with me?" Despair flared as the full impact of her mistake flooded through her. "We've been over this and over this and I put myself into a situation."

"Look, I'm sure he knows nothing is going on between you and Hunter."

But it probably hadn't looked that way. She had to explain what happened. "Any idea where he went?"

Savannah screwed up her face and looked everywhere but at Melody.

"What's going on? Where did Kyle go?"

"He might have hustled Hunter outside when you went back on stage."

"Which way?"

"Into the alley."

And with a curse, Melody headed for the stage door.

Eleven

As soon as Melody headed back on stage, Kyle grabbed Hunter and propelled him in the opposite direction. Rage dominated his emotions and fueled his strength as he made a beeline for the stage door. The kiss between Melody and Hunter had brought everyone of his fears to the surface.

She'd looked so damn happy in his arms. In those seconds before she'd shoved Hunter away, Kyle had been stripped down to the raw core of his psyche. In the instant that he'd watched another man swing a laughing, joyful Melody off her feet, every primitive elemental cell in his body had screamed for him to rip them apart and put his fist into Hunter's nose. And then the bastard had kissed her.

Even though he knew Hunter was the one to blame,

that Melody didn't love him, something tore inside Kyle. He hadn't done a good enough job loving her, hadn't given her everything he was, the good and bad. While he no longer feared losing her to Hunter, he wasn't sure he'd ever be able to win her love if he couldn't stop believing she'd leave him.

The heavy door gave beneath his onslaught, dumping the two men into the alley. A second later the door clanged shut, leaving them alone in the cool night air. At the far end of the alley a single light pierced the darkness, but where they stood it was as if the walls absorbed the light. The indistinct sounds of nearby traffic were barely audible over Kyle's harsh breathing.

"Where the hell do you get off kissing Melody?" he bellowed, his voice reverberating off the alley's walls. He shoved Hunter against the brick, venting every bit of rage and fury on the man.

"Screw you. You don't own her." Hunter's arrogant, conceited grin flashed in the dim alley. "Let me go."

"Why can't you just leave her alone?"

"Because she doesn't want me to." Hunter shoved at Kyle and bought himself enough breathing room to tear free.

Fists clenched, Kyle growled. "You're not going to get her back. She loves me. And that's my baby she's carrying. Plus, you don't strike me as the sort of guy who wants to play daddy."

"I could say the same about you."

"My wild days ended before Melody and I got together. We're going to be a family. She needs stability and consistency."

"Has it occurred to you that maybe she doesn't want what you're offering? Did you see her out on stage tonight? She's a star. She shouldn't have to settle for your limited vision of her as your wife and the mother of your kid."

Hunter's words came at Kyle with all the speed of a fastball and caught him off guard. That wasn't all he wanted for her. She deserved to have whatever career she wanted. And if that career took her away from him? True, the nine months they spent mostly apart while she was on tour had created an enormous rift in their relationship.

But should she be expected to give up her career for the sake of their family? Was that what he was pressuring her to do? Kyle thought over their last few conversations surrounding the future. She'd offered up vague answers about how she intended to promote her new album.

"This isn't any of your business," Kyle growled.

The stage door opened and Melody appeared. She took in the tense scene before stepping into the alley.

"What's going on?" She gazed from Kyle to Hunter.

Hunter spoke first. "I was just telling your boy here that you're too talented to take a step back from your career right now."

"Was he arguing with you?"

"He has some old-fashioned expectations when it comes to you."

"And you are setting him straight?"

Kyle repressed a grin at Melody's mild tone. Hunter had no idea how much trouble he was in at the moment.

It almost made Kyle feel sorry for him. Except he figured as soon as she was done with her ex-boyfriend, her sights would be set on him.

"Yes," Hunter said. "But I only have your best interest at heart."

"If that was true, you'd know that not only can I make my own decisions, but I've been doing a good job of it for a long time." There were icicles in her tone.

"I was merely trying to help."

Melody nodded toward the stage door. "If you don't mind, I'd like to speak to Kyle alone."

"Sure." With a quick glance in Kyle's direction, Hunter headed back into the club.

"Was that necessary?" she demanded as soon as they were alone.

"It felt pretty damned necessary to me."

"Why?"

He didn't understand how she'd managed to get him on the defensive. She was the one hugging and kissing her ex. "Do you seriously need me to answer that?"

"I rather think I do." She crossed her arms over her chest and fixed a steady, determined glare on him.

"You and Hunter."

"He hugged me. I hugged him back."

"He kissed you."

Some of her righteous anger dimmed. "I certainly didn't plan for that to happen. And maybe I shouldn't have hugged him, but I was excited."

"Has it occurred to you that you're encouraging him?" The accusation might not be fair, but Kyle couldn't hold it in.

"That's not true." She sucked in a shaky breath. "Okay, maybe it seems that way because he's been there for me a lot lately."

Kyle raked his fingers through his hair, struggling for calm as he absorbed her statement. "Meaning I haven't been?"

"Meaning Hunter and I have music in common and I value his opinions." This last she finished lamely as if she recognized that throwing her connection with Hunter in Kyle's face was sure to inflame their argument further.

"Did you know he was going to be here to introduce you tonight?"

"I didn't ask for him, if that's what you're thinking." She paused, and then said, "I'm pretty sure we're not fighting about Hunter."

"I'm pretty sure we are." He ground his teeth together. "I'm not accusing you of cheating."

"Well, thank goodness for that, because I wasn't and I haven't and I'm not going to."

"But it feels as if you like having it both ways."

"What is that supposed to mean?"

"You won't agree to marry me. Why is that?"

"Honestly, because you've never told me you love me."

"I do."

"And yet you can't bring yourself to say it. I get it, your father instilled in you the compulsion to repress your emotions because he thought they made you weak."

He had no argument and stared at her in frustration and anguish. His father had made him outwardly tough while his mother had made him inwardly weak. He could see every possible thing that could go wrong and it terrified him. But he couldn't bring himself to tell Melody that. She expected him to be strong, but being that for her also diminished his ability to be vulnerable.

She sighed and her voice calmed. "You say I want to have it both ways. I really only wanted one way. I want to feel safe in a relationship."

"That's why I asked you to marry me. I want you to realize that I'm committed to you and our daughter." Was there any better way to demonstrate how he felt about her than to make her his wife?

From Melody's expression, her consternation had grown as he spoke. "I don't want us to get married for the wrong reasons."

"We wouldn't."

"If I hadn't gotten pregnant, would you have asked me to marry you?"

"I believe we were heading there." He wouldn't have asked her to move in if he hadn't been going down that road. But he couldn't say for sure whether she'd been all that keen on the idea. "Or at least, I was."

"I don't believe you."

"I'm not the one who's skeptical about marriage. My parents might not be perfect for each other or even happy all of the time, but they've honored their vows and I don't doubt they'll stay married until death." Now it was her turn to answer some tough questions. "Did you see marriage in our future?"

"Honestly, I never imagined you'd ask me, so I never saw us married."

Her answer struck him hard even though it didn't surprise him. "Why were you with me at all?"

Her eyebrows rose in surprise. "You are fun and sexy, strong and sweet. You know how to make me laugh and can turn me on with a look. I enjoy being with you." She looked as if she wanted to say more, but then shook her head.

"That sounds like a description of how any number of men could make you feel. In fact, I think when I asked you what it was about Hunter that you couldn't live without, you said something similar."

"That's not true." But she frowned and he wondered if she was second-guessing herself.

"When I look at you," he said, "I see my future."

"How can you say that when you can't tell me you love me?"

"I have offered you everything I am. If three words are all that stands between us, then you can have them. Just don't be surprised when they don't bring you the happiness you expect."

Kyle paused, but it wasn't as if the words hadn't resonated through his thoughts a thousand times. He didn't want to say them like this. In the middle of a fight. To prove a point. He'd wanted the moment to be romantic and as perfect as he could make it. Yet, maybe love wasn't about the big moments, but rather the small ones.

He pulled in a breath, took control of his voice, and then spoke from his heart. "I love you."

* * *

I love you.

Damn him for being right.

Despite the truth in his eyes and the gravity with which he spoke the words, she didn't feel better. The problems between them weren't based on an unspoken declaration, but rather on unrealistic expectations. She'd thought that if Kyle broadcast his love for her, she would feel safe and secure. What she hadn't realized was that the true treasure of love was in being able to receive it.

And thus far, she'd proven herself a poor receptacle.

"You're right about needing to think," she said. "A little bit of time apart would be good for both of us."

For a split second he looked crushed by her decision and then he gave his head a sad shake. "I wasn't looking for more time apart. I think we've had too much of that already."

Once again she was the one retreating. What was wrong with her? The man had told her he loved her. She should be throwing herself into his arms and smothering him with kisses. Wasn't this what she'd been craving from him since the beginning? An admission of how he felt about her so she could feel protected?

"Look," he tried again. "We haven't done day twelve, communication, uninterrupted listening."

Had Kyle memorized the entire fourteen days' worth of exercises? It was infuriating that he remembered each activity, both the day and the detail. Melody couldn't seem to keep anything straight anymore. Before she finished her album, she'd blamed her lack of focus on that. Then she'd blamed the various changes her body was going through. The stress of potentially having a stalker. And this past week on rehearsing for the concert. But was any of that really the cause of her distraction?

"I just don't have the energy to talk or to listen right now," she said, knowing that for the last two weeks Kyle had been putting more effort into their relationship than she had. Maybe she wasn't good enough for him. Tears sprang to her eyes. She cursed the pregnancy hormones that made her want to cry at the worst times.

"That's fine," he said, his tone calm and reasonable. "We don't have to say another word. It's been a long week and you're exhausted. Let's go home. After a good night's sleep, both our heads will be clearer."

Except she didn't want to go home with him. She wanted to slink off somewhere and lick her wounds.

Aware that she was once again avoiding him when she should work on their relationship, she said, "I can't leave now. My friends came out to support me. Go if that's what you want to do."

And before he could answer, she turned on her heel and returned to the theater. She'd charged through the backstage area and reached the house before she noticed that Kyle wasn't behind her. She shouldn't be surprised. How many times could she push him away and expect he wouldn't get sick of it.

When she found Trent, Savannah, Nate and Mia, they'd been joined by Craig and a pretty blonde woman he introduced as Sasha. Savannah glanced in the direction Melody had come, obviously looking for Kyle, before shooting her a questioning look. Melody shook her head. Nate bought her a soda while Craig and Sasha congratulated her on the performance.

Her joy in the evening was severely reduced by the argument she'd had with Kyle and his subsequent absence. Had he gone home? Should she have gone with him?

The party started to break up after an hour, with Trent and Savannah leaving first. Melody walked into the lobby with the other two couples, hugging Nate and Mia before saying goodbye to Craig and Sasha.

She headed backstage to collect her purse and change into street clothes. Before she left the theater, she decided to give Kyle a call. She wasn't surprised when she got his voice mail and hung up without leaving a message. Obviously he was shutting down communications after she told him she didn't want to talk tonight.

On the way out to the parking lot, she dreaded the idea of returning to Kyle's house and risking another fight. Maybe she should just get a hotel room. Some space would probably be good for them. As she neared her rental car, she pulled out her phone and shot Kyle a quick text, letting him know her plan.

"You okay?"

Melody whirled around and spotted Craig approaching her across the lot. "I'm fine. I was just sending Kyle a text."

"How come he left?"

"He had another commitment tonight." She didn't want to get into the details with Craig. "Where's Sasha?" she asked, giving him a tired smile.

"She went home. We came separately."

"So where are you headed now?"

"Back to Las Vegas."

"Tonight?"

"Yeah, I drove down this morning to catch your show and now I'm heading back."

"You're driving?" As tired as she was, going home held a lot of appeal. She could be in her own bed by morning. "How long will that take?"

"About five hours."

"I was thinking about heading back to Las Vegas as well, but it's probably too late to catch a flight."

"You can ride back to Las Vegas with me," Craig said.

"I'm so tired, I doubt I'd be much company. And I have to drop my rental at the airport."

"I could follow you there."

"Okay." This was crazy. She should just find a hotel or better yet, go back to Kyle's house. But something elemental was driving her to run.

Maybe she was overwrought or just too tired to think straight, but an hour and a half later they were clear of LA and she was staring out the window at the darkness of the desert, her mind strangely numb. With her album done and her future with Kyle up in the air, she felt like a bit of dandelion fluff caught in a breeze, blown this way and that. She had no idea what she planned to do when she got back to Las Vegas or what she intended to do about her relationship with Kyle.

After last night, one thing was clear. If she didn't stop running he might give up chasing her. And judging by his lack of response to her earlier text, maybe he already had.

Twelve

Melody woke to daylight and blinked her eyes. As she lifted her head from the passenger-side window, her neck screamed in pain. She rubbed at the cramped muscles. It took her blurry mind a few seconds to orient her to their location. Still on I-15, moving parallel to the Strip. She glanced at the dashboard clock and saw that it was close to seven.

They'd stopped in Barstow for gas and something to eat, giving Craig an opportunity to rest and load up on coffee. Once back on the road, she'd been unable to keep her eyes open and managed a couple hours of sleep. But it wasn't enough. When she got back to the guesthouse, she intended to crawl into bed and sleep the rest of the day.

"How'd you sleep?" Craig asked.

"Not bad."

"Another twenty minutes and you'll be home."

"I can't wait." Silence filled the car as Melody yawned. "I know I already said this, but it was really nice of you to drive all the way to LA to hear me sing at The Roxy." She chuckled. "Especially when you hear me singing all the time."

"It's different when it's a concert. You have no idea how much you shine on stage, do you?" His eyes lingered on her, bright and filled with admiration.

"You're right about singing being different in front of an audience," Melody said, her gaze returning to the road ahead of them. "The energy was fantastic last night. Over the last few weeks, I'd been considering giving up my singing career and just going back to songwriting. But last night gave me hope."

"I suppose Kyle would prefer that you quit performing."

"No. He's always been supportive of my career."

But he had shared his concern about her going on another major tour like the one with Nate now that she was going to be a mom. And in truth, she couldn't imagine leaving her baby for any extended period of time. Yet, life on the road would be hard on kids with the constant moving from one city to the next.

"You shouldn't stop singing. You could be a great star."

"That's never been one of my goals. I love music, but there are sacrifices involved with becoming famous. You give up your privacy." She supposed that was already the case since she'd started dating Kyle.

He had a pretty high profile lifestyle as a former pro baseball player and partner in the LA Dodgers.

"It must be hard having so many people love you."

"I don't know about love me." She gave a self-conscious laugh. "I like to think they love my music."

"But you're so wonderful," Craig went on. "Not only are you incredibly talented, but you're really nice. People around the studio are always talking about how you know everyone's name and how you help people out all the time."

He was making her sound a lot more impressive than she actually was. It was a little embarrassing.

"That's sweet of you to say. I guess I remember what it was like starting out. If it wasn't for Nate I wouldn't have considered singing professionally. He encouraged me to get on the stage. How can I not pay that forward?"

"It's more than just that. You are a truly kind and thoughtful person."

Melody needed to turn the conversation away from her. "I really enjoyed meeting Sasha. You two make a very cute couple."

"We're not dating." Craig's voice had gone cold.

"Oh, I thought you were." Melody shook her head in bemusement. Sasha mentioned they'd been going out for a year. Maybe Craig was like Hunter and taking Sasha for granted. "She's really nice. And she really seems to like you."

"She isn't the woman I want." He smiled at Melody.

Suddenly she became aware of a certain sort of vibe coming off Craig and it made her a bit uncomfortable.

She'd always thought that Craig liked her, but now she wondered if his feelings for her were more involved than she'd realized.

"You might want to sit down and have a conversation with her," Melody said, knowing how hard that could be for both parties. "She seems to think you guys have a future together."

"She's wrong." There was rising irritation in his clipped tone.

Perhaps she'd pushed too hard. "Sure. Of course."

Since there didn't seem to be anything else to say, Melody lapsed into silence. As Craig made a left-hand turn, she realized she hadn't given him any directions since the first one. And yet he seemed to know exactly where he was going. She frowned. She'd given him the address to Trent's house. Had he fed it into his phone without her noticing? Her thoughts had been caught up in what she'd left behind in LA.

She started to pull the gate key out of her purse, but Craig rolled down his window and waved a card over the electronic lock. The gate arm began to rise.

"You have a key?"

"My aunt has a house in here. When you mentioned it, I recognized the name."

Had she mentioned the name of the gated community to him? She could have. Her brain had been pretty scattered these last few weeks.

Or maybe she was just being paranoid. Wasn't it possible that he'd heard things in passing from conversations she'd had at the studio with Nate?

"In fact, if you wouldn't mind a quick detour, I need

to pop in and check on the place. Water her plants. Look around to make sure nothing's wrong."

All Melody wanted to do was get home and crawl into bed, but Craig had been kind enough to drive her home. The least she could do was accompany him on a brief check of his aunt's place.

"Sure. As long as it's a quick stop." She hid a mighty yawn behind her hand. "Sorry."

"I get it. You've had a busy few months. What you need is to take some time off and rest. I can't imagine all the stress you've been under is good for the baby."

"You, Nate, my brother and Kyle. Everyone's worrying too much. I'm fine. The baby's fine. And it's early. It would be different if I was in the last month or two of my pregnancy."

Craig pulled into the driveway of a large home similar in size to Trent's. "This is my aunt's place."

Melody glanced around and recognized where she was from her frequent walks around the neighborhood. "Wow! She and my brother are really close. His house is a couple doors down on the street behind this one." In fact, she guessed there'd be a partial view of Trent's backyard from the second floor here.

"You don't say." Craig gave her a friendly smile and turned off the engine. "Would you mind helping me? Plant watering will go faster with a second set of hands."

"Sure." Anything to get this task done sooner.

Craig led her inside and toward the kitchen. As with Trent's house, the open floor plan offered unob-

structed views of the pool and the beautifully landscaped backyard.

"This is a really nice house," she said as she took a
watering can and headed for the plants near the stairs.
"What did you say your aunt does for a living?"

"She sells real estate in LA."

"So this is a vacation property for her?"

Craig nodded. "She likes to gamble and Las Vegas
is a quick flight."

While Craig headed upstairs, Melody poured three
cans of water on the plants downstairs. She was drag-
ging by the time she slipped the watering can back
under the sink. She cast out for some sign of Craig,
but couldn't hear him. This quick errand was stretch-
ing out longer than she expected.

"Craig?" she called out. "Are you about done?"

When she didn't hear anything she wandered into
the formal living room just off the foyer and perched
on the closest chair to the door. Her lashes drooped.
She rubbed her knuckles over her eyes. In another
five minutes she would fall asleep right where she sat.

"Craig," she tried again. This was ridiculous. She
was just around the corner from Trent's house. She
would just walk home. "I'm going to get going. I'll
just walk. Thanks for the ride."

Silence greeted her. While half of her wondered
what had become of him, the other half was burning
with frustration. She headed out to the car, but when
she tried the door handle, she realized it was locked.
Unable to get her bag out, she returned to the house.

"Craig?" She headed up the stairs and was halfway

to the top when she heard a sound coming from below. Turning, she spied him. "There you are. Look, if you still need to do things around here, I can walk home. I just need to get my bag out of your car."

"Why don't you stick around? I'll make us something to eat."

"I'm really tired and not very hungry." And growing more irritated by the second. "I just want to go home."

"Just a little while. Please."

As she retraced her steps down the stairs, he moved to cut off her exit through the front door. His demeanor was casual and relaxed, but for some reason the hair on Melody's arms stood on end. Why wouldn't he let her go?

"I'm really tired." She couldn't see a way to get past him and reach the front door.

"Please sit down."

"I don't want to sit down. I want to go."

He advanced toward her and Melody backed up. He herded her into the living room and gestured toward the couch. During her earlier assessment of the backyard, she'd noted that there was a tall concrete wall around the entire area. No way to escape there. She'd just have to play along until he decided to take her home.

"I am afraid I can't let you," he said.

Exhaustion and anxiety were blocking her ability to think clearly. "Why?"

"You need someone to take care of you and as you pointed out, you don't listen when people tell you to slow down and take care of yourself and the baby. So I'm going to do that."

How could he look so rational and say such outrageous things?

"What are you talking about?"

"You liked everything, didn't you?" His smile was overly personal. "The roses. The baby gift?"

Fear burrowed into her muscles, rendering them useless. "That was you?"

"Yes. I wanted you to know how much I love you."

"Those were very nice things, but you shouldn't have sent them. I'm with Kyle." Only she wasn't with Kyle. She had left him in LA. And come back to Las Vegas with Craig. And now she was in terrible trouble.

"In time you'll see he wasn't good for you. Not the way I will be. We are going to be so happy."

Kyle sat on the couch in his LA home and stared at the phone in his hands, willing Melody to call or text him back. He kept going back to her last message about spending the night in a hotel and cursing himself for not responding right away. At the time, he'd been so damned angry that he'd been afraid of what he might write back. But as night dwindled into morning, he'd sent her an apology and asked for her to call him as soon as she could. Now, lunch had passed without any response and his anxiety prompted a call to Trent.

"Have you and Savannah heard from Melody since last night?" Kyle said after Trent picked up.

"No. Haven't you?"

"She left me a text last night saying she was spending the night at a hotel. I've called her several times today, but she's not picking up." Maybe he shouldn't expect her to given the way they'd left things last night. She'd made it pretty clear she needed some time to think. "Could one of you try her?"

"Savannah's trying right now. Have you checked with Nate?"

"I haven't called him yet. He and Mia were heading to visit his mom in Texas. They left first thing this morning. They should've arrived by now."

"Savannah said she's not picking up."

Or she can't. Kyle banished that thought from his head. She was fine. It was all a case of him overreacting. But there was a sick feeling twisting in his gut. Why hadn't she reached out to anyone?

This was all his fault. He never should've let her walk away. Had something happened to her? Kyle supposed the next step would be to check the hospitals, but he was sure if there had been an emergency, he or Trent would have been notified.

"Could that security friend of yours in Las Vegas run her credit cards? Maybe we could figure out what hotel she's staying at." If Kyle knew where she was staying he could stop worrying.

"You don't think that's a little extreme?"

"May I remind you that someone sent her a teddy bear with a camera in it. Not to mention that her being out of contact for this long is unusual."

Trent paused for a couple seconds after considering Kyle's words. "I'll give Logan at Wolfe Security a call."

Feeling no less agitated despite their plan, Kyle shot Nate a message and then began to pace. Twenty minutes later, Trent called back.

"Logan ran her credit cards, and got a hit on a couple charges in Barstow. One of those was at a gas station. Which wouldn't be unusual if she drove back to Las Vegas, except it seems she turned in her car at LAX last night."

"She turned in her rental, but she didn't get on a plane." How had she gotten to Barstow? "What's going on?"

"What if she had her wallet stolen?" Trent suggested.

"Then she wouldn't have been able to get a hotel room and I'm sure she would've called you or Savannah."

"Maybe she got a ride from someone back to Vegas."

"Who?" And why would she do something like that? Especially without telling anyone? Kyle grabbed his keys and headed for the door. "I'm catching the first available flight to Vegas. It has to be where she was going."

"Are you sure you're not overreacting?" Trent asked.

Was it crazy to think something might have happened to her? That her stalker had tracked her down in LA and kidnapped her? Maybe this was all just a huge misunderstanding, but Kyle's gut told him something was wrong.

Kyle shook his head. "There are too many weird things going on."

After a brief pause, Trent asked, "Should we call the police?"

And tell them what?

"I want to," Kyle said. "But it hasn't been forty-eight hours and Nate hasn't responded to my text or voice mail. As soon as I hear from him, I'll let you know. In the meantime, can you send me Logan's number?"

By the time Nate called back half an hour later, Kyle had spoken with the security expert and had been reassured that they'd check into video footage from the Barstow gas station and send a car to Trent's Las Vegas house to see if she'd arrived there. Despite Logan's calm demeanor and crisp efficiency, Kyle wasn't at all reassured.

"Neither Mia nor I have heard from her," Nate said. "How long has she been missing?"

"She texted me last night that she was heading to a hotel. That was around midnight." He went on to explain how Logan had tracked her credit card to LAX and then Barstow. "It's as if she's heading back to Vegas by car. We just don't know the exact circumstances."

The slow pace of traffic on I-405 south had given him ample time to work himself into the beginnings of an anxiety attack.

Nate latched onto Kyle's concern. "You're thinking she's been abducted?"

"I'm thinking the logical explanation is whoever's

been stalking her finally made his move." Kyle let that sink in for a second. "It's not like her to disappear without saying anything to anyone."

"No, it's not. Have you thought about calling the cops?"

"Yes, but she hasn't been gone long enough for them to start looking for her."

At the moment, Kyle was regretting not reporting the previous strange incidents to the cops, but with all the crime that happened in Las Vegas every day, who could say if they'd even look into something as obscure as a few anonymous gifts?

Damn it. He never should've left her alone last night. He'd thought she was safe in LA. What had possessed her to take off for Vegas without saying anything to anyone? It just wasn't like her, making the possibility that she'd been kidnapped much more likely.

One thing was clear. He'd failed her, and that was completely unacceptable. No matter what the cost, he would do everything in his power to get her back.

Thirteen

Melody perched on the edge of the living room couch and contemplated her situation. Craig was obviously not ready to let her leave and she was not going to be able to get away from him. But he couldn't be vigilant all the time. At some point he would have to sleep or leave her to go to work and that was when she could escape.

Of course, the problem was what he intended to do with her in the meantime.

"I knew you and I were meant to be together the first time I heard you sing," Craig said, smiling at her with all the eager enthusiasm of an ardent lover.

"Craig, you know that I'm with Kyle." It was nearly impossible to keep the fear out of her voice, and she worried how he'd react if she got hysterical.

"He isn't going to be able to make you happy the way I can."

"Maybe not," she said, wondering how a seemingly normal guy could turn into a stalker. "But I love him."

"I don't think you do. You were leaving him after all."

She'd been so wrong to confide in Craig. "I just needed some time to think."

"Think about what?" Craig frowned. "He accused you of cheating on him."

"How did you know that?" She thought about the nanny cam teddy bear Kyle had found and barely repressed a shudder.

"I heard it around. That's why I knew he didn't deserve you. A woman like you would never cheat on the man she loves."

"No, but you mentioned that you saw the picture the paparazzi took of Hunter and me." Melody forced herself to say. "You could see where in the moment we looked like we were together."

"That's because Hunter wants you back."

Damn. The guy knew way too much about what was going on between her and Kyle. Was the teddy bear the only thing he'd bugged? She shuddered.

Craig continued, "He went to New York when you were there to see if there was a chance."

"That's crazy." Melody knew she'd chosen the wrong word when Craig's eyes widened. "What I meant to say was that Hunter didn't come to New York to see if we could get back together. He knew I was in love with Kyle."

"Yes, but you were in love with Hunter once, too."

Melody shook her head. "I only thought I was in love with Hunter. Once I started seeing Kyle, I understood that I was following a pattern with Hunter. Being with him stirred up the same insecurity that my father makes me feel. Growing up, my father barely had any time for me. I was always seeking his love and approval. I equated love with deprivation. Kyle's love made me stronger not weaker."

As much as she disliked digging out her emotional baggage for this virtual stranger, Melody sensed that keeping him talking was going to be the best way to convince him to let her go.

"Your dad is a terrible person. I've worked with several artists who used to be on the West Coast Records label. They told stories about how he ruined careers of people who tried to stick up for themselves. And I don't think he was any better with his own family."

Again, Craig knew way more than the average person. "How do you know all that?"

"I listen. Sometimes I record stuff. You'd be surprised what goes on in the studio when no one's around."

Melody's thought scrambled through the hundreds of hours she'd logged at Ugly Trout's studios. What sorts of things had she talked about in the recording booth, imagining herself safe? Some of that time Melody had spent with Mia, sharing romantic angst in the days before Mia and Nate had sorted out their issues. Melody suspected Nate would be furious at what his employee had done.

"Why would you do that? Those were private conversations."

"I need to know what's going on. The last two places I worked went out of business and I wasn't prepared to be out of a job. I swore that wouldn't ever happen again. I wanted to make sure I knew exactly what was going on at Ugly Trout."

"Why would you record me?"

"It wasn't you specifically. I just bugged the studios."

Melody noticed Craig had grown agitated as she put him on the spot and needed to calm him down. "Okay, I get it. Being out of a job is really scary and I promise if you let me go that I won't tell anyone."

"I'm not sure I believe you." Craig regarded her with a frown. "You'll need to stay here for a while."

"How long?"

"Until I know I can trust you."

Here were her worst fears realized. "How long do you think that will take?"

It was on the tip of her tongue to ask how he intended to keep her here, but she wasn't sure she wanted to put that question to the test. What if he tied her up or locked her in a room?

Her mind began to work overtime. She'd left LA without telling Kyle where she was going. He knew she was upset with him. How long before he'd wonder where she'd gone? Based on what had happened after the paparazzi incident with Hunter, it might be a couple weeks before he cooled off. And the argument in the alley last night had been so much more damaging than the previous incident because she'd pushed back.

But, even if she couldn't count on Kyle to look for her, surely Savannah, Trent or Nate would check in and after not finding her, start to worry. Should she warn Craig that this might happen in hopes that he'd let her go? Or would it backfire and her situation become even more dire?

"I don't know." Craig looked less confident and his expression grew more menacing. "I really want us to be together. I guess once I know you love me as much as I love you, then I can trust you."

His words roused her panic. How was she supposed to prove that she loved him? Would he expect her to sleep with him? A chill swept through her. Would he force her if she refused?

"I'm not feeling very well," she said, overwhelmed by the need to put a door between her and Craig. "Can I use the bathroom?"

"Are you sick?"

"Just morning sickness from being pregnant."

"Oh, sure. I've heard of that."

Wonderful, Melody thought, feeling nausea starting for real. "The bathroom?"

He pointed the way and she gratefully escaped to a small powder room. To her dismay, Craig camped outside the door and continued talking to her through the door.

"How long do the symptoms last? It's almost noon. Does that mean you'll stop feeling sick?"

"It depends. Sometimes I don't feel well all day."

She sat down on the closed toilet seat and dropped her head into her hands. "And it's worse if I don't have anything in my stomach."

"I don't have any food in the house."

"Could you go get something? It would really help."

"I don't want to leave you here alone."

"I'll be fine."

After a long pause, he said, "I gotta take care of something. I'll be back in a minute. Don't come out until I tell you to."

Afraid of the consequences if she disobeyed him, Melody sat in the bathroom and glanced between the closed door and her watch as the seconds ticked by. Where had he gone? It would be too much to hope that he'd left her alone in the house. Dare she make a break for it?

Summoning all her courage, she opened the door a crack. The sound of drilling came from somewhere in the large house. The bathroom door had muffled some of the sound. The pounding of her heart had blocked the rest. While he was occupied, she should make a break for the front door. It couldn't be more than thirty feet from where she stood to freedom.

But before she'd taken more than three steps, the drilling sound stopped. Melody glanced up, but couldn't see Craig. Did she still have time to make a break for it? Terror gave her the strength to try.

She had her hand on the front door knob and was turning it when Craig spoke.

"Where do you think you're going?"

"I just wanted some fresh air. Sometimes that makes me feel better."

"I think you're trying to leave. You can't do that." He seized her wrist, hard enough to bruise, and twisted her hand off the knob.

"You're hurting me," she protested, yanking her arm back in an effort to free herself. "Let me go."

He was strong, but adrenaline raged through her, fueled by her narrow escape. She kicked out at him, continuing to demand that he release her. Panic took ahold of her, turning her into a mindless, desperate animal. She needed to get away.

And then he let her go. Melody had a moment of searing relief before the left side of her face exploded in blinding pain. The impact of his hand against her cheek sent her stumbling backward. Her shoulder struck the wall leading into the living room and sent more pain blasting through her body.

Her father had struck her once. Not long after her mother had left. Melody had gone into a frenzy at the realization that she was being left behind and had screamed at her father, blaming him. At first he'd argued back, telling her to shut up and then to go to her room. But she'd been wild with grief and afraid of being abandoned. Looking back, Melody could barely remember what had been the exact trigger that caused her father to lash out and strike her.

It was all a blur of fear and pain. She'd never forgiven him, but probably as he'd intended, she respected his authority from that moment until she left LA to attend Juilliard at age eighteen.

"You made me do that," Craig said, grabbing her arm and pulling her toward the stairs.

Melody refused to respond. Her face stung, but she kept her spine straight, unwilling to let him know how hurt and afraid she was. This was not the moment to aggravate him further.

Instead, she retreated to that same place inside her where she'd gone the day her father had hit her. She went there to survive and plan.

As Kyle stepped out of the gangway and into the Las Vegas airport, he received a text from Melody.

Everything is fine with me. Not ready to talk yet.

This should've eased his mind, but he couldn't shake the anxiety as he texted her back.

Where are you?

Staying at a hotel. I don't want to see you.

And right there he knew it wasn't Melody.

His phone rang as he was contemplating how to respond. It was the security expert, Logan Wolfe.

"We've got her at that Barstow gas station with someone," Logan said to Kyle. "We're having trouble reading the license plate on their car, but we have a good picture of both Melody and the guy she's with from a camera inside the station. I'm texting a photo to you. Do you recognize him?"

Kyle glanced down at his phone's screen and saw the photo. It was off security footage and not the best quality, but something about the guy seemed familiar. One thing was clear: Melody wasn't afraid of the guy.

"I don't. I'll forward the photo to Trent and Nate. Maybe they'll have better luck. In the meantime, I got a text from Melody saying she's okay, but I'm pretty sure she's not sending the message. She claims she's staying at a hotel."

"And we know she was on the road between LA and Las Vegas last night. You think it's the guy she's with?"

"It would make sense if he's got her." Kyle was surprised how steady he sounded.

Damn it. Who was this guy? When Kyle got ahold of him, he was going to put him down.

Kyle's hands shook as he sent off the photo to Trent and Nate and hoped they were both standing by.

"Thanks for all your help, Logan."

"We'll keep at the security footage. My guys have some pretty sophisticated software. Hopefully they'll make some progress on the license plate."

"I'll let you know if Trent or Nate recognizes the guy." Before he could sign off, he had a text back from Nate. "Wait a second. Nate says it's Craig Jameson. He's a sound engineer at his recording studio." Kyle tried to picture the guy and couldn't.

"We'll check him out and get back to you."

Kyle was staring at the picture when his phone lit up with Nate's number. He answered immediately. "Who is this guy?"

"Nobody. I mean he's totally normal. Dull even." Nate paused and Kyle could imagine him shaking his head, equally baffled. "I'm racking my brain, but can't think of a single instance when he said or did anything inappropriate. Around Melody or anyone else."

"So he just snapped?"

"We don't know that he did anything," Nate said, but he didn't sound all that convincing. "Logan thinks he and Melody drove back to Vegas together?"

"It appears as if they were friendly and she obviously feels comfortable with him." Kyle's gut tightened as he imagined what might've happened to Melody since. "Right before Logan called, I got a text from her claiming she's staying in a hotel."

"You don't think it's her?"

"No. I think it's this Craig guy."

"So, we're assuming he offered her a ride back to Las Vegas," Nate said, sounding puzzled. "And then we think he what? Kidnapped her? This just doesn't make any sense."

"Why would he have been in LA?"

"He was at The Roxy for her performance."

Kyle was liking this less and less. "So obviously he's interested enough in her to make that trip." Could Craig have been her stalker? The roses that showed up at the studio. The ultrasound video that disappeared and then reappeared at the studio. It made sense.

"We don't know that's the only reason he was in LA," Nate said. "Maybe he had something else to do and since he was there decided to catch her show."

"Why are you defending him?" Kyle demanded, fists clenching.

"I'm not. I'm just trying to look at this from all angles. We don't really know what's going on."

Acid ate into Kyle's gut. "I know that Melody is missing and Craig is the last guy she was seen with. That's good enough for me."

Nate's tone grew conciliatory. "Hey, I get it. We're all worried."

"Sorry." The breath Kyle hauled in didn't calm him, but he knew nothing would be gained by lashing out. "I didn't mean to take anything out on you."

"It's okay. You did the right thing getting Wolfe Security involved."

"From the way Trent talked, they can dig into whatever we need to find her."

"If you need any information on Craig, just call the studio and ask for Reggie. He can get into the personnel files. Whatever you need."

"I appreciate it."

Kyle hung up and stared around the airport gate area without seeing any of it. Curses rang through his mind as he contemplated what could possibly be happening with Melody right now. He began making his way to the exit. He couldn't just sit around and wait. He had to do something. The phone rang as he left the terminal and was heading toward the parking lot.

It was Logan, calling him back. "We've got the guy's address and phone number. We tried calling, but it rolls straight to voice mail. I have a three-man team heading over to his house right now. They'll let me know what they find."

"Should we call the cops?"

"At this point we don't have any evidence of a kidnapping. Let's see what my guys find. It's possible we're barking up the wrong tree."

Logan didn't say what Kyle was thinking. That time was of the essence if Craig actually had abducted Melody. The cops would be slow to investigate, especially with the question of whether or not she had a stalker. Roses and a nanny cam weren't all that conclusive.

"Give me his address," Kyle said. "I want to be there."

"That's not a good idea." Logan's tone brooked no argument. "Let my men handle it."

"Please tell them to be careful." Kyle could imagine too many ways this scenario could go wrong.

"Don't worry, they're trained in this sort of operation. Just sit tight and I'll let you know what they come up with."

Kyle couldn't just sit around waiting to hear. "That's not good enough. I need to be doing something."

"At this point there isn't much to do. I promise I'll let you know as soon as I hear anything."

Kyle headed to his car. He could go to Nate's studio and get Craig's personnel records. There'd be an emergency contact. That person might know something. And he could talk to the sound engineer's coworkers. Surely they would know something that could shed light on what made Craig tick.

Half an hour later, he was sitting in Nate's office

at Ugly Trout. Logan had called a couple minutes ago and said that they'd struck out at Craig's house. Kyle's jaw ached from clenching his teeth. The only thing keeping panic in check was a lifetime of repressing his emotions.

Before him on the desk was Craig's personnel file. He typed the guy's address into his phone, and then scanned through the paperwork for an emergency contact. Craig had listed his mother in California. Kyle dialed the number, unsure what he planned to say.

Hello, Mrs. Jameson. Do you happen to know where your son might have taken the woman I love?

When a woman answered, Kyle began the conversation with more tact. "Mrs. Jameson, my name is Kyle Tailor. I work with Nate Tucker at Ugly Trout Records where your son is employed and I was wondering if you've heard from Craig lately."

"Not since last week. Is something wrong? Has he been hurt?"

Not yet.

"Nothing like that. He isn't at work today and we had some questions for him. He's not answering his cell phone. He mentioned spending some time with a friend. Any idea where they might have gone."

"I don't know how I can help you. I haven't heard from him. Have you tried him at home?"

"Yes, it doesn't appear as if he's been there for a couple days. I believe he was in LA to see a concert last night and he was supposed to come back to Las Vegas sometime today." Kyle left out the part where he'd been caught on the gas station security footage in Barstow. "What I'm wondering is if he hasn't been home, maybe you know someplace else he might have gone."

"I can't imagine. Sometimes he likes to gamble at the casinos. Not that he's a big gambler or anything. Maybe that's where he is and he's turned off his cell phone."

"I guess if that's what he's done, then we're out of luck. Would you happen to know a favorite hotel he likes to gamble at?" It was a long shot, but it was possible that Craig had taken Melody to a hotel.

"No. I'm sorry. Oh, wait. My ex-husband's sister has a vacation home in Vegas. Craig looks after the place when they aren't using it. Waters the plants, makes sure the air-conditioning is working, that sort of thing."

"Would you happen to have the address?"

"No. I'm not on good terms with my ex's family. But I can't imagine Craig being there. Why would he when he has a perfectly nice home of his own?"

Why indeed. An empty house would be the perfect place to stash the woman you kidnapped.

"Maybe I can look up her address. What is her name?"

"Minerva Brooks. But I'm pretty sure she's not listed."

"I guess it never hurts to check." And Kyle had access to the sort of people who knew how to get information. "Thank you for your help."

As soon as Kyle hung up with Craig's mother, he called Logan. "I have the name of Craig's aunt. Minerva Brooks. She has a house in Las Vegas that he has access to."

Kyle heard the keys click while Logan input the name on his computer. "That's interesting. She has a house in the same gated community that Trent lives in."

Understanding lanced through Kyle. The mysterious gifts. The nanny cam with the short range. Melody had thought she was safe in the gated community, but her stalker had full access. Kyle cursed.

"That has to be where he has her."

"You sit tight." Logan's deep voice was edged with warning. "I'll send my guys over there."

"Sure."

But this time, Kyle didn't have to sit back and wait for Logan's men to make their move. He had a location, maybe not an exact address. The neighborhood wasn't all that extensive. How hard was it going to be to spot a couple black SUVs and a security team?

Fourteen

Like a caged tiger, Melody paced the bedroom Craig had locked her in. The afternoon had faded into evening, taking daylight with it. She stared out the window at the surrounding homes, so near and yet, thanks to the large lot sizes in the gated community, so far. As the western horizon had gone dark and lights began to appear behind the curtains of the nearby houses, she'd barely resisted the urge to throw open the window and start screaming for help.

She'd been afraid to draw Craig's attention. From the look of the padlock he'd affixed to her door, he had no intention of letting her escape. But he hadn't thought of everything. The bedroom was on the second floor and the drop to the ground was daunting, but she'd already decided she was less afraid of the height than staying in this house much longer.

But she had to wait. She didn't dare risk trying to escape while he was still in the house. He'd already demonstrated his willingness to punish her once. She was scared how far he'd take things if she tried and failed to escape a second time.

Her stomach growled. She hadn't eaten anything since they'd stopped in Barstow, over fifteen hours earlier. He'd said there was no food in the house so he had to go shopping at some point. He claimed he wanted to take care of her, so he wasn't going to let her starve. The problem with where the bedroom was situated in the house was that she couldn't see the driveway and determine if his car was still parked there. She'd spent some time with her ear pressed to the door, but couldn't hear anything.

After taking all this into consideration, she'd decided to make her break in the wee hours of the morning. Like the escapees in any good movie, she stripped the bed and made a rope of sheets she could tie to the bed leg and dangle out the window. To her relief Craig hadn't thought about nailing the window shut.

A quick glance at the clock radio on the nightstand showed her it was nearly seven in the evening. Had anyone wondered why she hadn't checked in? Nate had taken Mia to visit his mother in Texas this morning. They would be too busy to think about her. As for Trent and Savannah, Craig had her phone and could have texted them that everything was fine.

That left Kyle.

The way she'd treated him the night before, she wouldn't be surprised if he never wanted to see or speak to her again. Except that wasn't his style. Especially now that she was carrying his daughter. But how long before he reached out? And even if he did, what sort of vile messages would Craig send in her stead? Would Kyle believe them? She hadn't exactly fallen into his arms after he told her he loved her.

In the long hours that she'd paced this room, she'd realized just how stupidly she'd been behaving. Why hadn't she listened to Kyle when he told her that Hunter was interfering in their relationship? Damn. Why had she let Hunter kiss her? Kyle had every right to be furious.

She had so much to make up for. She only hoped when she got out of this mess, he would be willing to give her another chance.

A faint noise sounded downstairs. Melody began to realize how she'd attuned herself to the silence, searching for anything that would indicate Craig was still in the house, until she heard...voices? Someone was here. She ran to the bedroom door and began pounding on it. Were her frantic cries loud enough to penetrate the door and reach the people below? Regardless of who they were, surely they would be curious about the noise.

She barely heard the sound of the padlock being removed, but then the door was opening. Heart pounding, terrified that it was Craig and not someone who could help her, she retreated. When Kyle's face appeared in the opening, pale and haggard with worry, she covered her mouth and then rushed at him.

His arms came around her body, crushing the breath from her lungs. Burying her face in his neck she held on for dear life while he soothed her with gentle reassurances.

"It's okay," he murmured, stroking her hair. "You're safe."

"Where's Craig?"

"Some friends of mine are taking care of him downstairs."

"I can't believe you found me." It was hard to get the words out between gulping breaths.

"I'm sorry it took so long." His hands drifted up and down her back while his strong body absorbed her shaking. "Are you okay? He didn't hurt you, did he?"

She shook her head. "No. I'm fine."

As if not believing her claim, he held her at arm's length. His gaze immediately went to the side of her face where Craig had struck her. She put her fingertips over the spot and couldn't meet his eyes.

"Did he do that to you?"

"I'm fine. Really." She touched his face, her eyes pleading with his. "I love you. I'm so sorry for what happened last night."

"Last night?" He blinked as if he couldn't figure out what she was talking about.

"You told me you loved me and I ran away." She swept tears from her cheeks with the back of her hand. "Again. I've been so stupid. I love you."

"I love you, too." He cupped her face. "I've been in

love with you since that day at the bagel place when you twisted your ankle and I kissed cinnamon and sugar off your lips. I'm sorry I haven't told you that every day since."

He'd always treated her with such devoted affection. Why had it been so important for her to hear the words? How much heartache could've been avoided if she'd just believed they truly belonged together.

"Let's get out of here."

Melody nodded her agreement and let Kyle guide her down the stairs. Four large men dressed in impeccable black suits and black shirts watched her approach.

"These men are from Wolfe Security," Kyle explained as they neared the bottom.

One of them stepped forward as she and Kyle moved into the foyer. He stood significantly over six feet tall. "You okay, ma'am?"

"Fine." Melody couldn't help glancing at Craig.

He was seated on the floor in the archway that led to the living room, hands bound behind his back, staring into space. Melody shrank against Kyle as Craig glanced toward her.

"Make them understand I did it because I love you," he said.

She felt Kyle tense and dug her fingers into his arm. "Don't."

The muscles beneath her hand didn't uncoil as Kyle urged her toward the front door. When they got outside, Melody sucked in a lungful of night air.

"Come on," Kyle led her toward his car.

"What about the police?"

"The security team is handling that call. We'll wait for them out here."

Once she was tucked into the passenger seat of Kyle's car, the little bit of calm she'd achieved vanished and she began to shake in earnest. Kyle got behind the wheel and pulled her into his arms. Safe with him, she gave in to the overwhelming anxiety and fear that she'd bottled up these last terrifying hours.

By the time the police arrived, her trembling had subsided and she felt her strength coming back. Kyle handed her a packet of tissues for her to blow her nose. Smiling her gratitude, she dabbed away tears.

With her breathing finally under control, she said, "I must look a mess."

"You're the most beautiful thing I've ever seen."

Not only had the cops shown up, but also the paramedics. They checked her over and pronounced her okay except for elevated blood pressure, but because of the baby, they wanted her to go to the emergency room and be checked out. Before she left, the police took her statement and she got to hear how Kyle had found her with the help of Wolfe Security.

At the hospital, they photographed the bruise on her face and then checked out her and the baby. Both received a clean bill of health and Kyle took Melody back to his house. On the way, they swung through a drive-through and she wolfed down a hamburger and large fries in record time.

She was half-asleep by the time he tucked her into bed, but she seized his hand before he could move away.

"Please don't leave me," she said, tugging at him. "I need you."

To her relief, Kyle lay down beside her and pulled her into his arms. The steady beat of his heart beneath her cheek should've been enough to ease her into sleep, especially because the adrenaline of her misadventure had long ago worn off.

"I had a lot of time to think today," she told him. "I have made so many mistakes in the last few months. I don't want to make another one."

"We've both made our share."

Melody silenced him with a finger to his lips. "This last fiasco is on me. If I hadn't been so blind to Hunter's motives for spending time with me, and then not believed you've loved me all along, I wouldn't have run away from you in LA and ended up with Craig."

He grabbed her hand and kissed her fingers before pulling them away so he could speak. "I shouldn't have overreacted when I saw you with Hunter."

"I'm glad you did. I don't know why I've been so blind. I wanted you to say that you loved me, but I was too blind to see that if you didn't care, you wouldn't have been bothered that Hunter wanted me back." She paused. "And I set him straight, by the way. I told him you're my future."

"I love hearing that." Kyle sealed his vow with a reverent kiss.

"And I want that future to be in LA. I've had enough of Las Vegas." She gave a small shudder and snuggled closer.

"Oh." He sounded surprised.

"Oh?" She echoed, looking up into his face. "What?"

"When you seemed conflicted about where you wanted to live, I started looking for a house here."

"You don't want to move."

"No, but I thought we could go back and forth. With your family living here, I know you want to be close."

"Did you find a house?"

"I found three. I intended to get your opinion on them before I bought anything."

"Before *we* bought," she corrected him. "I think it's time I stopped renting and mooching and become a homeowner. I want this to be our home."

It was important to her that she'd realized it, but now that she'd said the words out loud, she wanted nothing more than to buy their home.

"I love that idea." He kissed her again. This time with focused passion, tempered by gentleness. "And can we go get married tomorrow? I don't care if you want to have a big wedding down the road, but right now there's nothing I want more than to make you my wife."

"I think that's a great idea." Coming so close to losing him a second time had finally driven home how much she adored him. "I don't need anything, but you."

And with a smile on her lips, she proceeded to show him exactly how much.

Epilogue

Day fifteen. Hire a professional photographer to take pictures of you as a beautiful memory of your commitment to and completion of this relationship revitalization challenge.

It took them ten months to reach the final exercise, but Melody had wanted a photo that reflected how blessed they were and insisted on including her entire family in the picture. Kyle had hired the same photographer who'd done Melody's album shoot and Nate and Mia's wedding photos. They were gathered at the home Kyle and Melody had bought in LA.

After Melody's abduction, she hadn't wanted to stay in Las Vegas any longer. She'd returned with Kyle to LA, only returning to Sin City to prepare for and then testify in Craig's trial. Both Kyle and Melody had decided that their new family needed a house with more yard for their daughter to run around and sold Kyle's Bird Streets house, opting for a sprawling Monterey colonial sitting on nearly a half acre with glorious gardens, sun-drenched rooms and a guesthouse.

Kyle balanced sleeping four-month-old Lily on his arm and watched Trent wrangle his active toddler back into the shot. Beside him, Melody let her head fall onto his shoulder. He felt as much as heard her soft sigh.

"Is ours going to be that bad?" Nate was on Kyle's other side, glancing from Trent and Savannah's bundle of energy to the bright-eyed infant in his wife's arms.

"I hope so," Mia murmured, kissing her son's bald head.

He'd been born a month premature after she'd displayed signs of preeclampsia and the doctor induced labor. Although there had been a few tense hours after Mia had been rushed to the hospital, Aiden Tucker had been born without incident. And to hear his father tell it, the boy was perfect.

"You hope so?" Nate asked his wife as Trent tucked Dylan under his arm and carried him—with loud protests and flailing interspersed with giggling—back to the photo shoot.

Mia sounded amused. "Boys are supposed to be active."

"There's active," Nate said, shaking his head in bemusement as Dylan settled like an angel onto his mother's lap after being promised a cookie, "and then there's wild."

"Chasing after him will keep you in shape," Kyle

said as Melody adjusted the bow in Lily's soft brown hair and smoothed the skirt of her pale pink dress.

He wasn't sure how he'd been blessed with two such beautiful women in his life, but he wouldn't trade his current happiness for all the no-hitters in the world.

"Are you sure you don't want me to take her?" Melody asked, unable to stop fussing over her daughter.

"You know I have this."

"You are the most awesome father ever." She gave him a wistful smile. "It's just that I'm going to be gone for two days and I'm going to miss her terribly."

"We could come with you," Kyle offered for the umpteenth time. "I can clear my schedule and we can all go up to San Francisco for your show."

"As much as I'd love that, I need to see if I can handle these short weekends away from you and Lily."

After releasing her first album, Melody had been booked into several small venues before her pregnancy advanced to a point where she complained that no one wanted to see a woman give birth on the stage. Once Lily was born, she'd let Nate talk her into performing three times over the course of three months. The first of those performances was this upcoming weekend.

"Maybe it would be better if you took both of us along and that way you will see we can make taking your act on the road work for our family."

Becoming a mom had inspired Melody and she'd been writing furiously for the last several months. Nate was encouraging her to get back into the studio. Mia was excited to produce her friend's music. So far Melody had refused to go forward while she and Kyle discussed how best to balance her career with their family life. Both were conscious of how an extended separation had affected their relationship last time. Kyle was confident that after the lessons they'd learned and the relationship work they continued to do each day, they wouldn't fall prey to the same problems this time around. Still, he wasn't all that keen on living without his wife or daughter for even a day.

Trent had taken a break from his business to spend several months on location with Savannah. There was no reason Kyle couldn't do the same. In fact, he was looking forward to watching his wife live her dream.

"You don't know how stressful all the travel can be," Melody said.

"I know exactly how it is. I spent twelve years in the majors and we were on the road half the time."

"You didn't have a baby to worry about."

"Are you kidding? I had a clubhouse full of big babies that were never happy," he joked. Seeing she wasn't convinced, he leaned down and kissed her lightly on the lips. "I want us to be together and I want you to become a huge star. Whatever I can do to help make that happen I will do."

Her eyes grew luminous. "Stop being so wonderful. I can't cry. It will ruin my makeup and we haven't taken a single picture."

"Is everyone ready?" the photographer asked.

This brought everyone's attention back to the business at hand. From his position behind Savannah, Trent and Dylan, Kyle beamed with pride and happiness. Next to him, Nate radiated a similar joy. How odd that a year ago all three owners of Club T's had been involved with the three women who sat or stood beside them, but each couple had been struggling to find their way.

Since then, Trent had released past hurts and reconnected with the only woman he'd ever loved. Nate had fought for and won the woman of his dreams. And Kyle had learned that sharing his deepest thoughts and emotions with Melody made his life so much richer and joyful.

"Thank you for making all my dreams come true," Kyle murmured to Melody as the photographer announced that he was done with the photo shoot.

"Your dreams?" Melody echoed in surprise. "I think it's me who's lucky to have you." She gazed down at their daughter. "Both of you. I never imagined I could be so happy."

"How about our dreams?" he countered. "You, me and our daughter. No matter what the future holds we are going to have each other."

Melody's eyes shone bright. "And it doesn't get better than that."

* * * * *

DANIEL PORTER SAT at the edge of the bed. Again and again he dismantled and rebuilt his Glock 17. Before he removed the magazine, he racked the slide to ensure no ammunition remained in the chamber. He lifted the upper portion of the semiautomatic, detached the recoil spring as well as the barrel. Then he put everything back together.

Rinse and repeat.

Some things you had to do over and over, until every cell in your body learned to perform the task on autopilot. That way, when bullets started flying, you'd react the right way—immediately—without having to check a training manual.

When his eyelids grew heavy, he placed the gun on the nightstand and stretched out across the mattress only to toss and turn. Staying at the Strawberry Inn without a woman wasn't one of his brightest ideas. Sex kept him distracted from the many horrors that lived inside his mind. After multiple overseas military tours, constant gunfights, car bombs, finding one friend after another blown to pieces, watching his targets collapse because he'd gotten a green light and pulled the trigger...his sanity had long since packed up and moved out.

Daniel scrubbed a clammy hand over his face. In the quiet of the room, he began to notice the mental chorus in the back of his mind. Muffled screams he'd heard since his first tour of duty. He pulled at hanks of his hair, but the screams only escalated.

This. This was the reason he refused to commit to a woman. Well, one of many reasons. He was too messed up, his past too violent, his present too uncertain.

A man who looked at a TV remote as if it were a bomb about to detonate had no business inviting an innocent civilian into his crazy.

He'd even forgotten how to laugh.

No, not true. Since his return to Strawberry Valley, two people had defied the odds and amused him. His best friend slash spirit animal Jessie Kay West... and Dottie.

My name is Dorothea.

She'd been two grades behind him, had always kept to herself, had never caused any trouble and had never attended any parties. A "goody-goody," many had called her. Daniel remembered feeling sorry for her, a sweetheart targeted by the town bully.

Today, his reaction to her endearing shyness and un-intentional insults had shocked him. Somehow she'd turned him on so fiercely, he'd felt as if *years* had passed since he'd last had sex rather than a few hours. But then, everything about his most recent encounter with Dot—Dorothea had shocked him.

Upon returning from his morning run, he'd stood in the doorway of his room, watching her work. As she'd vacuumed, she'd wiggled her hips, dancing to music with a different beat than the song playing on his iPod.

Control had been beyond him—he'd hardened in-stantly.

He'd noticed her appeal on several other occasions, of course. How could he not? Her eyes, once too big for her face, were now a perfect fit and the most amaz-ing shade of green. Like shamrocks or lucky charms, framed by the thickest, blackest lashes he'd ever seen. Those eyes were an absolute showstopper. Her lips were plump and heart-shaped, a fantasy made flesh. And her body...

Daniel grinned up at the ceiling. He suspected she had serious curves underneath her scrubs. The way the material had tightened over her chest when she'd moved...the lushness of her ass when she'd bent over... every time he'd looked at her, he'd sworn he'd devel-oped early-onset arrhythmia.

With her eyes, lips and corkscrew curls, she re-minded him of a living doll. *Blow her up, and she'll blow me.* He really wanted to play with her.

But he wouldn't. Ever. She lived right here in town. When Daniel first struck up a friendship with Jessie

Kay, his father expressed hope for a Christmas wedding and grandkids soon after. The moment Daniel had broken the news—no wedding, no kids—Virgil teared up.

Lesson learned. When it came to Strawberry Valley girls, Virgil would always think long-term, and he would always be disappointed when the relationship ended. Stress wasn't good for his ticker. Daniel loved the old grump with every fiber of his being, wanted him around as long as possible.

Came back to care for him. Not going to make things worse.

Bang, bang, bang!

Daniel palmed his semiautomatic and plunged to the floor to use the bed as a shield. As a bead of sweat rolled into his eye, his finger twitched on the trigger. The screams in his head were drowned out by the sound of his thundering heartbeat.

Bang, bang!

He muttered a curse. The door. Someone was knocking on the door.

Disgusted with himself, he glanced at the clock on the nightstand—1:08 a.m.

As he stood, his dog tags clinked against his mother's locket, the one he'd worn since her death. He pulled on the wrinkled, ripped jeans he'd tossed earlier and anchored his gun against his lower back.

Forgoing the peephole, he looked through the crack in the window curtains. His gaze landed on a dark, wild mass of corkscrew curls, and his frown deepened. Only one woman in town had hair like that, every strand made for tangling in a man's fists.

Concern overshadowed a fresh surge of desire as he threw open the door. Hinges squeaked, and Dorothea paled. But a fragrant cloud of lavender enveloped him, and his head fogged; desire suddenly overshadowed concern.

Down, boy.

She met his gaze for a split second, then ducked her head and wrung her hands. Before, freckles had covered her face. Now a thick layer of makeup hid them. Unfortunate. He liked those freckles, often imagined—

Nothing.

"Is something wrong?" On alert, he scanned left… right… The hallway was empty, no signs of danger.

As many times as he'd stayed at the inn, Dorothea had only ever spoken to him while cleaning his room. Which had always prompted his early-morning departures. There'd been no reason to grapple with temptation.

"I'm fine," she said, and gulped. Her shallow inhalations came a little too quickly, and her cheeks grew chalk white. "Super fine."

How was her tone shrill and breathy at the same time?

He relaxed his battle stance, though his confusion remained. "Why are you here?"

"I…uh… Do you need more towels?"

"Towels?" His gaze roamed over the rest of her, as if drawn by an invisible force—disappointment struck. She wore a bulky, ankle-length raincoat, hiding the body underneath. Had a storm rolled in? He listened but heard no claps of thunder. "No, thank you. I'm good."

"Okay." She licked her porn-star lips and toyed with the tie around her waist. "Yes, I'll have coffee with you."

Coffee? "Now?"

A defiant nod, those corkscrew curls bouncing.

He barked out a laugh, surprised, amazed and delighted by her all over again. "What's really going on, Dorothea?"

Her eyes widened. "My name. You remembered this time." When he stared at her, expectant, she cleared her throat. "Right. The reason I'm here. I just… I wanted to talk to you." The color returned to her cheeks, a sexy blush spilling over her skin. "May I come in? Please. Before someone sees me."

Mistake. That blush gave a man ideas.

Besides, what could Miss Mathis have to say to him? He ran through a mental checklist of possible problems. His bill—nope, already paid in full. His father's health—nope, Daniel would have been called directly.

If he wanted answers, he'd have to deal with Dorothea…alone…with a bed nearby…

Swallowing a curse, he stepped aside.

She rushed past him as if her feet were on fire, the scent of lavender strengthening. His mouth watered.

I could eat her up.

But he wouldn't. Wouldn't even take a nibble.

"Shut the door. Please," she said, a tremor in her voice.

He hesitated but ultimately obeyed. "Would you like a beer while the coffee brews?"

"Yes, please." She spotted the six-pack he'd brought with him, claimed one of the bottles and popped the cap.

He watched with fascination as she drained the contents.

She wiped her mouth with the back of her wrist and belched softly into her fist. "Thanks. I needed that."

He tried not to smile as he grabbed the pot. "Let's get you that coffee."

"No worries. I'm not thirsty." She placed the empty bottle on the dresser. Her gaze darted around the room, a little wild, a lot nervous. She began to pace in front of him. She wasn't wearing shoes, revealing toenails painted yellow and orange, like her fingernails.

More curious by the second, he eased onto the edge of the bed. "Tell me what's going on."

"All right." Her tongue slipped over her lips, moistening both the upper and lower, and the fly of his jeans tightened. In an effort to keep his hands to himself, he fisted the comforter. "I can't really tell you. I have to show you."

"Show me, then." *And leave.* She had to leave. Soon.

"Yes," she croaked. Her trembling worsened as she untied the raincoat…

The material fell to the floor.

Daniel's heart stopped beating. His brain short-circuited. Dorothea Mathis was gloriously, wonderfully naked; she had more curves than he'd suspected, generous curves, *gorgeous* curves.

Was he drooling? He might be drooling.

She wasn't a living doll, he decided, but a 1950s pinup. *Lord save me.* She had the kind of body other women abhorred but men adored. *He* adored. A vine with thorns and holly was etched around the outside of one breast, ending in a pink bloom just over her heart.

Sweet Dorothea Mathis had a tattoo. He wanted to touch. He *needed* to touch.

A moment of rational thought intruded. Strawberry Valley girls were off-limits…his dad…disappointment… But…

Dorothea's soft, lush curves *deserved* to be touched. Though makeup still hid the freckles on her face, the sweet little dots covered the rest of her alabaster skin. A treasure map for his tongue.

I'll start up top and work my way down. Slowly.

She had a handful of scars on her abdomen and thighs, beautiful badges of strength and survival. More paths for his tongue to follow.

As he studied her, drinking her in, one of her arms draped over her breasts, shielding them from his view. With her free hand, she covered the apex of her thighs, and no shit, he almost whimpered. Such bounty should *never* be covered.

"I want…to sleep with you," she stammered. "One time. Only one time. Afterward, I don't want to speak with you about it. Or about anything. We'll avoid each other for the rest of our lives."

One night of no-strings sex? Yes, please. He wanted her. Here. Now.

For hours and hours…

No. No, no, no. If he slept with the only maid at the only inn in town, he'd have to stay in the city with all future dates, over an hour away from his dad. What if Virgil had another heart attack?

Daniel leaped off the bed to swipe up the raincoat. A darker blush stained Dorothea's cheeks...and spread... and though he wanted to watch the color deepen, he fit the material around her shoulders.

"You...you don't want me." Horror contorted her features as she spun and raced to the door.

His reflexes were well honed; they had to be. They were the only reason he hadn't come home from his tours of duty in a box. Before she could exit, he raced behind her and flattened his hands on the doorframe to cage her in.

"Don't run," he croaked. "I like the chase."

Tremors rubbed her against him. "So...you want me?"

Do. Not. Answer. "I'm in a state of shock." And awe.

He battled an insane urge to trace his nose along her nape...to inhale the lavender scent of her skin...to taste every inch of her. The heat she projected stroked him, sensitizing already desperate nerve endings.

The mask of humanity he'd managed to don before reentering society began to chip.

Off-kilter, he backed away from her. She remained in place, clutching the lapels of her coat.

"Look at me," Daniel commanded softly.

After an eternity-long hesitation, she turned. Her gaze remained on his feet. Which was probably a good thing. Those shamrock eyes might have been his undoing.

"Why me, Dorothea?" She'd shown no interest in him before. "Why now?"

She chewed on her bottom lip and said, "Right now I don't really know. You talk too much."

Most people complained he didn't talk enough. But then, Dorothea wasn't here to get to know him. And he wasn't upset about that—really. He hadn't wanted to get to know any of his recent dates.

"You didn't answer my questions," he said.

"So?" The coat gaped just enough to reveal a swell of delectable cleavage as she shifted from one foot to the other. "Are we going to do this or not?"

Yes!

No! Momentary pleasure, lifelong complications.
"I—"

"Oh my gosh. You actually hesitated," she squeaked. "There's a naked girl right in front of you, and you have to think about sleeping with her."

"You aren't my usual type." A Strawberry Valley girl equaled marriage. No ifs, ands or buts about it. The only other option was hurting his dad, so it wasn't an option at all.

She flinched, clearly misunderstanding him.

"I prefer city girls, the ones I have to chase," he added. Which only made her flinch again.

Okay, she hadn't short-circuited his brain; she'd liquefied it. Those curves...

Tears welled in her eyes, clinging to her wealth of black lashes—gutting him. When Harlow Glass had tortured Dorothea in the school hallways, her cheeks had burned bright red but her eyes had remained dry.

I hurt her worse than a bully.

"Dorothea," he said, stepping toward her.

"No!" She held out her arm to ward him off. "I'm not stick thin or sophisticated. I'm too easy, and you're not into pity screwing. Trust me, I get it." She spun once more, tore open the door and rushed into the hall.

This time, he let her go. His senses devolved into hunt mode, as he'd expected, the compulsion to go after her nearly overwhelming him. *Resist!*

What if, when he caught her—and he *would*—he didn't carry her back to his room but took what she'd offered, wherever they happened to be?

Biting his tongue until he tasted blood, he kicked the door shut.

Silence greeted him. He waited for the past to resurface, but thoughts of Dorothea drowned out the screams. Her little pink nipples had puckered in the cold, eager for his mouth. A dark thatch of curls had shielded the portal to paradise. Her legs had been toned but soft, long enough to wrap around him and strong enough to hold on to him until the end of the ride.

Excitement lingered, growing more powerful by the second, and curiosity held him in a vise grip. The Dorothea he knew would never show up at a man's door naked, requesting sex.

Maybe he didn't actually know her. Maybe he should learn more about her. The more he learned, the less intrigued he'd be. He could forget this night had ever happened.

He snatched his cell from the nightstand and dialed Jude, LPH's tech expert.

Jude answered after the first ring, proving he hadn't been sleeping, either. "What?"

Good ole Jude. His friend had no tolerance for bull, or pleasantries. "Brusque" had become his only setting. And Daniel understood. Jude had lost the bottom half of his left leg in battle. A major blow, no doubt about it. But the worst was yet to come. During his recovery, his wife and twin daughters were killed by a drunk driver.

The loss of his leg had devastated him. The loss of his family had changed him. He no longer laughed or smiled; he was like Daniel, only much worse.

"Do me a favor and find out everything you can about Dorothea Mathis. She's a Strawberry Valley resident. Works at the Strawberry Inn."

The faint *click-clack* of typing registered, as if the guy had already been seated in front of his wall of computers. "Who's the client, and how soon does he— she?—want the report?"

"I'm the client, and I'd like the report ASAP."

The typing stopped. "So this is personal," Jude said with no inflection of emotion. "That's new."

"Extenuating circumstances," he muttered.

"She do you wrong?"

I'm not stick thin or sophisticated. I'm too easy, and you're not into pity screwing. Trust me, I get it.

"The opposite," he said.

Another pause. "Do you want to know the names of the men she's slept with? Or just a list of any criminal acts she might have committed?"

He snorted. "If she's gotten a parking ticket, I'll be shocked."

"So she's a good girl."

"I don't know what she is," he admitted. Those corkscrew curls…pure innocence. Those heart-shaped lips…pure decadence. Those soft curves…*mine, all mine*.

"Tell Brock this is a hands-off situation," he said before the words had time to process.

What the hell was wrong with him?

Brock was the privileged rich boy who'd grown up ignored by his parents. He was covered in tats and piercings and tended to avoid girls who reminded him of the debutantes he'd been expected to marry. He preferred the wild ones…those willing to proposition a man.

"Warning received," Jude said. "Dorothea Mathis belongs to you."

He ground his teeth in irritation. "You are seriously irritating, you know that?"

"Yes, and that's one of my better qualities."

"Just get me the details." Those lips…those curves… "And make it fast."

CAN'T HARDLY BREATHE—available soon from Gena Showalter and HQN Books!

COMING NEXT MONTH FROM

Available October 3, 2017

#2545 BILLIONAIRE BOSS, HOLIDAY BABY
Billionaires and Babies • by Janice Maynard
It's almost Christmas when Dani is snowed in with her too-sexy boss—and an abandoned baby wearing a note that says he's the father! Nathaniel needs Dani's help, but playing house means finally facing the desire they can no longer deny...

#2546 BILLIONAIRE'S BABY BIND
Texas Cattleman's Club: Blackmail • by Katherine Garbera
Amberley knows better than to fall for another city boy, but widowed tech wizard Will has an infant daughter who makes her heart melt! When the chemistry between Amberley and Will won't quit, will he open his heart once more to love?

#2547 LITTLE SECRETS: SECRETLY PREGNANT
by Andrea Laurence
Cautious Emma cut loose once—*once*—at a party, only to find herself pregnant by her masked lover. She meets him again in the last place she expects...at work! He's the rebellious CEO of the company she's auditing. Now can she avoid mixing business with pleasure?

#2548 FIANCÉ IN NAME ONLY
by Maureen Child
Brooding celebrity writer Micah only wants to be alone with his work. But somehow his gorgeous neighbor has tempted him into the role of fake fiancé! Now pretend emotions are becoming real desire. So what happens when their time together comes to an end?

#2549 THE COWBOY'S CHRISTMAS PROPOSITION
Red Dirt Royalty • by Silver James
Quincy Kincaid's vacation is almost within reach, until a baby is abandoned with a country superstar! She has every intention of resisting the sexy singer—until they're trapped together for the holidays. Now all she wants for Christmas is him...

#2550 ONE NIGHT STAND BRIDE
In Name Only • by Kat Cantrell
Playboy Hendrix Harris never calls a woman twice. But after the scandal of a public Vegas hookup, the only solution is to settle down—with a convenient marriage. But Roz makes him want more than temporary... So how will he let her go?

Get 2 Free Books,

Plus 2 Free Gifts—

just for trying the Reader Service!

HARLEQUIN *Desire*

SPECIAL EXCERPT FROM

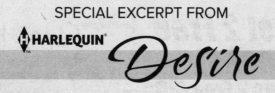

HARLEQUIN
Desire

*It's almost Christmas when Dani is snowed in with her
too-sexy boss—and an abandoned baby wearing a note
that says he's the father! Nathaniel needs Dani's help,
but playing house means finally facing the desire they
can no longer deny...*

Read on for a sneak peek of
BILLIONAIRE BOSS, HOLIDAY BABY
by USA TODAY *bestselling author Janice Maynard,
part of Harlequin Desire's #1 bestselling*
***BILLIONAIRES AND BABIES** series.*

This was a hell of a time to feel arousal tighten his body.

Dani looked better than any woman should while
negotiating the purchase of infant necessities during the
beginnings of a blizzard with her brain-dead boss and an
unknown baby.

Her body was curvy and intensely feminine. The
clothing she wore to work was always appropriate, but
even so, Nathaniel had found himself wondering if Dani
was as prim and proper as her office persona would
suggest.

Her wide-set blue eyes and high cheekbones reminded
him of a princess he remembered from a childhood
storybook. The princess's hair was blond. Dani's was
more of a streaky caramel. She'd worn it up today in a
sexy knot, presumably because of the Christmas party.

HDEXP092017

While he stood in line, mute, Dani fussed over the contents of the cart. "If the baby wakes up," she said, "I'll hold her. It will be fine."

In that moment, Nathaniel realized he relied on her far more than he knew and for a variety of complex reasons he was loath to analyze.

Clearing his throat, he fished out his wallet and handed the cashier his credit card. Then their luck ran out. The baby woke up and her screams threatened to peel paint off the walls.

Dani's smile faltered, but she unfastened the straps of the carrier and lifted the baby out carefully. "I'm so sorry, sweetheart. Do you have a wet diaper? Let's take care of that."

The clerk pointed out a unisex bathroom, complete with changing station. The tiny room was little bigger than a closet. They both pressed inside.

They were so close he could smell the faint, tantalizing scent of her perfume.

Was it weird that being this close to Dani turned him on? Her warmth, her femininity. Hell, even the competent way she handled the baby made him want her.

That was the problem with blurring the lines between business and his personal life.

Don't miss
BILLIONAIRE BOSS, HOLIDAY BABY
by USA TODAY *bestselling author Janice Maynard,*
available October 2017 wherever
Harlequin® Desire books and ebooks are sold.

www.Harlequin.com

HDEXP092017

EXCLUSIVE
Limited Time Offer

$1.⁰⁰ OFF

New York Times Bestselling Author

GENA SHOWALTER

returns with an irresistible
Original Heartbreakers story!

Can't
**HARDLY
BREATHE**

Available August 29, 2017.
Pick up your copy today!

HQN™

$7.99 U.S./$9.99 CAN.

$1.⁰⁰ OFF the purchase price of CAN'T HARDLY BREATHE by Gena Showalter.

Offer valid from August 29, 2017, to September 30, 2017.
Redeemable at participating retail outlets. Not redeemable at Barnes & Noble.
Limit one coupon per purchase. Valid in the U.S.A. and Canada only.

52615027

5 65373 00076 2   (8100)0 12299